A FEAST OF SONGS

In an act of kindness, Ellie offers to look after her friend's great aunt Phyllis after she suffers a fall. She travels to East Anglia and is entranced by the seaside town of Fairsands, as well as the handsome and charming shopkeeper and restaurateur, Joe. Instead of the relaxing time she was hoping for, though, Ellie finds herself the target of acts of sabotage. Thinking revenge is the motive, she suspects Joe's former girlfriend Amber. But is she really a *former* girlfriend . . . ?

PATRICIA KEYSON

A FEAST OF SONGS

Complete and Unabridged

LINFORD
Leicester

First published in Great Britain in 2014

First Linford Edition
published 2014

A catalogue record for this book is available
from the British Library.

ISBN 978–1–4448–2225–0

Published by
F. A. Thorpe (Publishing)
Anstey, Leicestershire

Set by Words & Graphics Ltd.
Anstey, Leicestershire
Printed and bound in Great Britain by
T. J. International Ltd., Padstow, Cornwall

This book is printed on acid-free paper

1

Ellie cleared away the supper things and spread out the holiday brochures she'd collected during her lunch hour. Somewhere exotic looked nice, but she knew it would be expensive. No harm in dreaming though, she thought as she flicked through the pages of Land Rovers amidst big game and beautiful women enjoying spa treatments or taking colourful cocktails on sun-bleached beaches. Another year perhaps.

She skimmed through the pages on family holidays — no good to her, they were more suited to her friend Susan and her brood. That Spanish break looked good, but there was the inevitable single supplement; as if it wasn't bad enough that you had to go on your own, let alone pay extra for the privilege. It was no good. She could find nothing suitable.

'We've booked our family holiday at Eurodisney in Paris,' bragged Susan at work the next week. 'Mum's coming and she'll look after the kids while Kev and I get some time to do grown-up things.'

'Paris,' sighed Ellie. 'How romantic.'

'That's what Kev said,' giggled Susan.

'I hope you have a lovely time,' said Ellie. She tried to smile. She was pleased they had found the holiday they wanted, but wished she had a nice break to look forward to as well. If she'd been given a choice, she wouldn't have booked leave from work, but her line manager had more or less told her to take it, so she had put in the request. Now she'd acclimatised herself to the idea of a vacation, she felt she'd be happy to do anything as long as she got away for a while. Well, maybe not camping in a muddy field.

'But you're off the same week as me,' said Susan. 'Are you going anywhere?'

'I expect I'll find somewhere,' replied

Ellie. But she felt destined to stay at home with nothing interesting to do. She imagined spending the week running around doing chores for her flatmates.

May came around quickly and Susan was jumping around the office like an animated puppy. 'I can't wait until Saturday,' she declared. 'The children are excited and even Mum's looking forward to France.'

Susan's enthusiasm was infectious and the two friends were soon chatting about the Eurodisney site. And, of course, gay Paree.

On Saturday morning, Ellie phoned Susan to wish her a good holiday, but her phone was constantly engaged. She got through just before lunchtime. 'What's up?' she asked. 'I've been trying to wish you a nice time in Paris.'

'Doesn't look as if we'll be going,' wailed Susan. 'Mum's ancient aunt has had an accident and she lives alone. There's no one to look after her.'

'Poor soul,' said Ellie. 'But even if

your mum stays behind, you, Kev and the children can go, can't you?'

'I couldn't go without Mum,' Susan assured her. 'It wouldn't seem right. Anyway, she paid for the tickets, you know.'

Ellie didn't know, and things fell into place now. She'd wondered how Susan and Kev had managed to afford an expensive holiday when they usually appeared to be in debt. 'I could look after your ancient relative,' she volunteered.

There was a moment's silence at the end of the phone, then, 'Why would you?' asked Susan.

'Because I've got a week's holiday from work and nowhere to go,' laughed Ellie. As she thought about it, the idea of going somewhere and having a purpose was starting to grow on her. She could hear Susan shouting something to someone in the background, presumably relaying the good news that the holiday could still be on.

'I'll ring you back in half an hour. You're the best, Ellie.'

* ★ ★

And that was why Ellie was driving towards East Anglia on Saturday afternoon, quite looking forward to her unexpected holiday adventure. She refused to consider the down sides if they were there; of course she'd get on with Susan's mother's ancient aunt and of course she'd find things to do even in East Anglia. Travel hopefully, that was her motto.

Arriving at the hospital, she found Phyllis Dewar sitting in a chair by a bed. She was a tall, square lady, nothing like Ellie had imagined her to be. She was dressed in slacks and a cardigan which was buttoned up unevenly around a plastered left arm. Ellie tried not to let her horror show as she surveyed the livid bruises on Phyllis's face. She must have taken quite a tumble.

Ellie introduced herself and received an acknowledgement.

'I've asked the nurse to make a list of

things for you to do,' Phyllis said. 'It's Ludo I'm anxious for.'

'Ludo?' Ellie thought the old lady might have lost her memory or something as she wasn't sure what she was talking about.

'My dog,' said Phyllis impatiently. 'Didn't they tell you anything?'

Ellie hadn't a clue a dog was involved. She knew nothing about them and hoped it wasn't a snarling, snappy type. She plucked the piece of paper from the bed and looked at it. 'You seem to have thought of everything,' she said. 'If you'll let me have a key I'll go and find Ludo and get the shopping you need.'

'I expect to be discharged in the morning. Come and collect me at ten.' And Ellie was dismissed.

She found Auntie Phyllis's cottage quite easily. She let herself in and was greeted by a wet nose and a half-hearted lick from an old brown and white Springer Spaniel. 'Hello, Ludo,' she said, bending to stroke him. 'Don't worry. I'm supposed to be here. I'm not a burglar.' Ludo gave her hand another little lick before ambling off to the sitting room to resume his wait for the mistress of the house.

Ellie dragged in her belongings from the car and did a tour of the little cottage, which didn't take long. Two rooms and a kitchen downstairs, and two bedrooms and a bathroom upstairs. It was obvious which was Phyllis's bedroom, so she went into the smaller back room and unpacked her things. It was a pleasant room and she looked out of the window down into the tiny garden area, which was an array of colourful pots and garden ornaments. To one side she noticed a raised bed with what looked like vegetables growing in it.

Remembering her duties towards the old dog, Ellie went downstairs and fed him. He was a lovely animal and Ellie warmed towards him, admitting to herself that his mistress was a bit of a cold fish. 'Come on, Ludo,' she encouraged, unhooking the lead from the back of the door. 'Walkies.'

He didn't look too keen, but he hadn't been out all day and Ellie could do with a walk as she'd been in the car a long time. She shrugged on her fleece and the two of them set off to explore.

Ellie hadn't realised Phyllis lived so near the sea and it was wonderful to wander along the seafront listening to the waves shushing across the pebbles as they ebbed and flowed. She took a deep breath, letting the salty air soothe her. It would be all right — it was only for a week, and what else would she be doing?

Sitting in front of the television with a mug of cocoa beside her, Ludo asleep across her feet, Ellie suddenly remembered the shopping she should have got. Too late now, she supposed. There would hardly be anywhere open in this small town at such a late hour. Perhaps she ought to find out.

She was in luck. A small corner shop was open and she was able to pick up milk, bread and something for lunch the next day. She wasn't a great cook, but she could manage a passable chicken casserole. An apple pie and a tub of ice cream were added to her basket before she went to pay.

'On holiday, are you?' asked the chap at the till. 'Haven't seen you before, that's all. I would have remembered.' He grinned.

'I'm staying with Phyllis Dewar,' replied Ellie, returning the smile. She'd already noticed his curly brown hair and bright, twinkling blue eyes. 'Do you know her?'

'Oh yes, everyone knows Phyllis. Is she all right now? I hear she had a fall.'

'She comes out of hospital tomorrow and I'm going to be looking after her for the week,' said Ellie. As an after-thought, she asked, 'Is there anything special Phyllis buys?'

'Cream,' he replied. 'She likes double cream. I see you've already chosen her favourite apple pie.'

Ellie added a pot of cream to her

basket. 'I'm Ellie, by the way, and it looks as if I might be a regular customer — for this week anyway.'

'And I'm Joe.' His smile was broad and Ellie found herself grinning back.

With the shopping safely stowed in Phyllis's kitchen, she settled down for a bit more television with Ludo. Joe was a nice young man. Something about him appealed to her even after such a short acquaintance. She'd have to visit his shop more often.

* * *

Once at the cottage, Phyllis hurried to get out of the car and into the house. 'Ludo,' she shouted. 'He's deaf, but I expect you realised that. Ludo! I'm back. Oh there you are, you dear thing. Have you missed me?'

The old dog's tail thumped his reply and his wet tongue licked Phyllis's face as she bent to fondle him. Here was another side of Phyllis which Ellie was relieved to discover. Obviously she'd been worried about the dog and had been missing his company.

'I'll make some tea, shall I?' Ellie offered after ensuring Phyllis was in the big comfy armchair in the sitting room with Ludo at her feet. Without waiting for permission, she disappeared into the kitchen, returning when the tea was ready.

Phyllis waved at the mug dismissively. 'I won't drink that.'

Ellie decided it was best to ignore the comment. 'I'll cook a chicken casserole for lunch. Is there anything I can get you before I make a start?'

'There was roast chicken on the menu at the hospital. If I'd known I was going to have to make do with a stew I'd have stayed there a bit longer.'

Swallowing down an acerbic reply, Ellie went back to the kitchen and cut up the chicken rather more viciously than was necessary, adding some vegetables she'd found in the fridge and some herbs. Keeping out of Phyllis's way for as long as possible seemed a good plan, so she cleaned the kitchen.

'What are you doing?' Phyllis was standing in the doorway staring at her. 'Anyone would think I'd been away for a week instead of overnight.' Without waiting for a reply, she lifted the lid of the saucepan. 'I won't eat much of that.'

'Fine,' replied Ellie, her voice rising in a strangle. 'I paid for it out of my own money, so I don't suppose you'll mind if I have some. I haven't eaten since last night.' She put away the cleaning cloth and asked, 'Shall I take Ludo out now? There's just about time for a short walk before lunch.'

'Yes, he'll need to be walked. Not too far, mind.'

Ellie took down the lead from behind the door and Ludo ambled towards her. 'Good boy. Let's have a nice walk. We can go down to the sea again, can't we? See if there are any seagulls to chase.'

Phyllis made a humphing sound and returned to her chair. Ellie decided not to care as, if push came to shove, she could always leave — just walk away. It was the dog she felt sorry for.

After a bracing walk along the seafront, Ellie knew the rest of the day would hang heavily and if ever chocolate was needed, it would be then. Instead of turning for Phyllis's cottage, she went to the shop she'd visited the previous evening. She hoped Joe would be in the shop and was happy to see him serving another customer when she arrived. It didn't take long to gather up the items she wanted.

'Oh dear, that looks serious,' laughed Joe when he saw her basket full of chocolate bars.

'Definitely serious,' Ellie replied. 'That woman is no joke!'

'What do you mean? Phyllis is all right. A bit obstinate at times, but nothing too bad.'

Ellie decided she'd better keep quiet. After all, Joe knew Phyllis much better than she did. Perhaps they'd just got off on the wrong foot. She hoped things would improve. Time would tell.

Phyllis sat at the dining table pushing the chicken around with her fork.

'At least it's your left hand which you hurt,' said Ellie, trying to make conversation.

'I'm left-handed.' Phyllis fixed her with a steely glint.

She had to be, thought Ellie.

Phyllis pursed her lips and speared a piece of meat with her fork. They sat in silence and Ellie noticed that Phyllis ate quite a bit of the meal, forking it into her mouth quite adeptly when she thought Ellie wasn't watching.

'Joe said you liked apple pie and cream.' Ellie carried a dishful towards the table and put it down in front of Phyllis.

'He's a nice young man,' was the reply.

While Ellie cleared away and washed up, Phyllis sat with Ludo in the sitting room.

'Would you like to come with us when I take Ludo out later on?' asked Ellie.

'I won't be able to walk, will I?'

Once again, Ellie bit back a reply. 'I'll go up to my room then and take Ludo out later. Is there anything you need before I go up?'

'I've all I want here.' Phyllis stroked Ludo's ears.

* * *

Up in her room, Ellie eyed the chocolate bars with relish, but somehow she didn't feel like ripping one open and devouring it. She found a couple of books which took her interest on a shelf in the bedroom and immersed herself in one of them. Before she knew it, her watch told her it was nearly teatime. Scrambling off the bed, she raced down the stairs to put the kettle on. Phyllis must be parched. Ellie knew she should be encouraging her to drink as part of the recovery process.

Phyllis was in the kitchen struggling to fill the kettle. 'I was thirsty. Where were you?'

15

'I got engrossed in one of the books in my bedroom,' explained Ellie. 'It was about garden ghosts.' She laughed. 'Have you got one?'

'Oh several, I shouldn't wonder.' Phyllis showed no sign of having made a humorous comment.

'Let me fill the kettle. Would you like something to eat with your cup of tea?'

'I prefer coffee. I'm not hungry.'

That's what she said at lunchtime, thought Ellie. She dashed upstairs and brought down the fun-sized treats she'd bought at Joe's shop. Placing them on a tray with the drinks, she carried it through to the sitting room.

Ludo's nose twitched and Phyllis picked up her coffee. 'I like a cup and saucer, but I see you've used a mug.'

'I thought it would be easier to manage as you've only got one hand working at the moment.' She smiled as Phyllis drank her coffee and absent-mindedly helped herself to some chocolate.

'If you like we could take the car to

16

the seafront and you could get a breath of air,' offered Ellie.

Phyllis's eyes registered interest, but she said, 'No, I'll stay here. It's been a harrowing day for me. Anyway, I should sort out some clothes which are easy to get in and out of. I'll do that while you're out with Ludo.'

Ellie was pleased to escape and Ludo was a willing companion. The poor old dog wasn't up to Ellie's fast pacing, so she slowed to make the walk more convivial. By mutual consent they headed towards the sea and Ellie was pleased to see Joe's shop open.

'Hi,' she called. Joe grinned at her. 'Me again. I forgot to ask Phyllis about dog food for Ludo. Should I buy some, do you think?'

'I deliver it to her. She has quite a few tins at a time and they're stored in the shed. I don't think a delivery is due just yet, but I'll take a look.'

Ellie was impressed by the attention he gave his customers. It was a world away from her usual shopping experience at the supermarket. 'You work very hard. Are you open all day, every day?'

'It often seems like that.' Joe laughed and leant on the counter. 'It's my dad's shop and we like to please our customers.' He shrugged. 'To tell you the truth, there's not an awful lot to do down here, even in the summer. I don't mind hard work.'

That was one thing they had in common at least. Ellie hoped she would get the chance to find out more about him, but for now she had no further excuse to stay in the shop.

'I'm trying to persuade Phyllis to get some sea air, but she doesn't appear too keen.'

'I expect that fall knocked her confidence. She usually likes to walk along the seafront and pop into the shop. Tell her I said hi.'

* * *

'Joe from the shop wishes to be remembered to you,' said Ellie, trying to be tactful with her wording.

Phyllis almost smiled. 'That's an odd expression for him to be using. He's usually more informal than that.'

'What he actually said was, 'Tell her I said hi.' '

'That's more like Joe.'

'I think I'll make some sandwiches for us and then feed Ludo. Is that all right with you, Mrs Dewar?' Ellie had been debating for ages how she should address Phyllis and she hoped she'd got it right.

'There's a tin of salmon in the cupboard and I see you bought some bread. Ludo's food is in the shed if there aren't any more tins left by the back door.'

* * *

The three of them ate well at suppertime and Ellie was feeling more optimistic about the time ahead. 'I am

19

happy to help you with any personal care you can't manage,' she said, having rehearsed the words carefully. 'But you must let me know what you'd like me to do.'

'I shall need help to undo this dress and I might not bother with underwear. Is that dreadful of me?'

'Not at all. Very sensible given the circumstances. I'll put the chair from my room near the washbasin in the bathroom, shall I? That should make it easier for you to have a wash.'

Phyllis stood up and headed towards the stairs. Unexpectedly, she swayed and Ellie had to be quick to catch her or she would have fallen again. 'It's all right, Mrs Dewar, I've got you.' She hoped she sounded more confident than she felt. Gently, she lowered Phyllis onto a chair in the hallway. A knock on the door startled them both.

'Hi,' smiled Joe. 'Whoa, how about those trendy new specs, Phyllis. They're dazzling.'

'Talk about a knight in shining

armour,' said Phyllis. 'Park your white horse and come in. What are you here for?' Ellie was amazed at the sparkle of interest Joe had conjured up in Phyllis; she almost appeared to be flirting with him.

'To see you, of course.' Joe winked at Ellie. 'That, and to return Ellie's notebook which she left in the shop.'

Ellie liked his manner with the older woman. Together Joe and Ellie saw Phyllis upstairs and left her lying on the bed.

'Thanks, Joe. I don't know how I would have managed if you hadn't come by.'

'It was more of an excuse to see you than anything else. Although, of course I wanted to return your notebook.' Ellie felt her face growing hot. 'I also wanted to ask if you'd come for a drink or something while you're here,' continued Joe. 'But it looks as if Phyllis needs more than a little TLC. I've never seen her look so upset.'

Joe loped off up the road and after

struggling with her feelings Ellie went back upstairs to see how Phyllis was. It was hard to concentrate when Joe had just asked her out for a drink.

'I feel all right,' Phyllis said, struggling to sit up on the bed. 'But when I start walking around I sort of lose my bearings.'

Trying to cheer her up, Ellie said, 'Joe was right about your glasses. They're rather splendid. Are they new?'

'Yes, only had them a day or two.' She closed her eyes and let out a shuddering sigh. 'I think I'd better get ready for bed. Thank you for all your help, Ellie. I'm sorry I was a bit cranky, but I was worried about what would happen if I couldn't manage on my own.'

'Well you're not on your own. I'm here.'

With Phyllis settled in bed, Ellie went into her own room and looked out of the window. A lot had happened on this strange day. Thinking back over the events, she wondered if she might have the answer to Phyllis's problem.

2

Despite her excitement in hoping she could help Phyllis, Ellie slept well and woke to the smell of coffee. Quickly she scrambled out of bed, pulled on her robe and went downstairs. Phyllis was in the kitchen.

'Mrs Dewar, I wish you'd be careful coming down the stairs on your own. You weren't too well yesterday.'

Phyllis treated her to a sour look which took Ellie aback considering how pleasant she had become the previous evening. 'I came down very cautiously,' she assured Ellie. 'If I can't manage to go up and down stairs on my own, I might as well go into the old folks' home.' Her lips tightened into a thin line. Phyllis refilled her coffee mug and shuffled towards the sitting room.

Ellie followed, ignoring the fact that

she hadn't been invited to help herself to a drink. 'I expect your optician thought it would be easier for you to have just the one pair, is that it? My gran has one pair for reading and another for distance. She gets fed up changing them over.'

Phyllis plonked herself into her armchair and Ludo wandered over to sit at her feet. 'You're not going to let this go, are you? I hope there's a point to your questioning, but yes, what you say is correct. My old pairs are over there.' She gestured towards a shelf.

Ellie crossed her fingers and brought the old spectacles over. Gently she took the coffee from Phyllis and put it on the table beside her. Then she asked her to stand up. Phyllis opened her mouth, but promptly shut it again and did as she was told. As soon as she was upright, she swayed and plopped down into her chair again. She put her hand to her forehead and said, 'I feel a bit dizzy. Do we have to do this?'

'Let's swap your glasses,' said Ellie.

'Are these your distance ones?'

Phyllis peered at them and then nodded. She put them on when Ellie held them out to her.

'Can you stand up again, please?' Ellie instructed.

'I don't know. I don't want to fall.'

'I won't let you. Promise.' Ellie held out her arms towards Phyllis and encouraged her to stand.

'That was better. The room didn't go round that time.' Phyllis walked towards the window, brushing aside Ellie's helping hands. She looked down, then up and then out of the window. 'What sort of a trick have you pulled?'

'No trick,' Ellie assured her. 'Your new glasses are very attractive, but they're bifocals, aren't they? It's my guess you're using the reading bit of the lenses for distance and it's distorting your vision and making you dizzy.'

Phyllis returned to her chair and popped her glasses on and off, on and off. 'You're right. Oh, Ellie, I'm indebted to you. Thank you.'

'I think you should check with the optician, though,' said Ellie. 'You probably need a new prescription for those glasses.' She pointed towards the two older pairs. 'You could still get something trendy.'

Phyllis laughed. 'That's the least of my concerns now.' She lifted her coffee mug and took a sip. Then she looked at Ellie shyly. 'I'm sorry for being brusque. I was so worried.'

'I'll make myself a drink and then I'll get you some breakfast, Mrs Dewar,' replied Ellie, heading for the kitchen.

'I think you could call me Phyllis, don't you, dear?'

In the sanctuary of the kitchen, Ellie punched the air and let out a sigh. Thanks to her gran's experience, she had guessed what Phyllis's problem could have been. If there had been any serious health problem, the hospital would have picked it up, she felt sure.

* * *

'I can manage, I'm not helpless,' Phyllis said as Ellie hovered round her ready to lend a hand. 'I'll call if I need you.' Phyllis shut the bathroom door firmly.

Nevertheless, Ellie hung around on the landing hoping everything would be all right.

At last they were downstairs again and Ludo was sniffing around, lumbering between the door and his mistress.

'I'll take him out, Phyllis, shall I?' Ellie wanted to persuade Phyllis to go as well, but didn't want to press the point. She had been through quite a bit of disruption in the last couple of days and she didn't want to add to it.

'Yes, he'll want a walk. Where were you thinking of going?'

Ellie hadn't actually thought of anywhere, but now she did, the corner shop was inviting. 'We need something for our meals today. Anything you fancy?'

'I could come with you. You won't

have a clue what to get otherwise, I don't suppose.' Phyllis was already on her feet.

Ellie hid a smile. 'If we're going shopping, I'd better take the car. Will you mind? We can still have a walk along the seafront if we feel like it.' Was that a look of relief in Phyllis's eyes? One step at a time.

Ellie parked the car as near the shop as she could. 'Do you want to wait here? I've got the list you made before we left home.'

'I'm coming in with you. Got to let Joe see I'm all right and to thank him for helping yesterday. It was good of him to visit. He'd be a good catch for some lucky young woman.' Phyllis hauled herself out of the car and Ludo, having raised his head hopefully, settled down once more on the back seat, his head resting on his front paws.

'Phyllis,' called Joe. 'Be with you in a minute. Why not take a seat while you wait. Your glamorous young assistant can wait on you.'

Taking the hint, Ellie took a basket and inspected the shelves. 'What sort of bread do you prefer, Phyllis?' she enquired. 'Brown or white?'

'White. Although what you bought the other day wasn't bad. Are there any soft rolls? We could freeze some.'

'And cheese? Do you like cheese? Or we could get some ham?'

'It's on the list.' Phyllis shook her head.

Oops, thought Ellie. She'd only been trying to involve Phyllis in the decision-making. Perhaps it would be better just to get the stuff. And then she would have time to chat with Joe if she was lucky. The shop was filling up, though.

All hopes of a private conversation with Joe flew out of the window by the time she arrived at the counter.

'We're going for a walk along the front,' Phyllis informed him. 'And I wanted to ask if you'd like to come to supper this evening.'

★   ★   ★

29

With Ludo on a lead and Phyllis hanging onto her other arm, Ellie said, 'What was that about Joe coming for supper? Is it a private party? I can take sandwiches up to my room if so.'

Phyllis grinned. 'We'll have the sandwiches when we get back and then we'll get cracking on the supper. What shall we make?'

'We've got mince,' said Ellie. 'Spaghetti bolognese?'

'Too messy for me,' declared Phyllis. 'Cottage pie?'

'Is that Joe's favourite?'

'It's mine.'

'I used the veg from the fridge. Shall I go back to the shop and get some? They weren't on the list.' Ellie frowned, trying to remember if they had been, but she was sure they weren't.

'We'll get *them* from the garden,' replied Phyllis. 'Now let me sit on that seat and you carry on with Ludo. Collect me on your way back.'

★ ★ ★

Ellie and Phyllis spent an enjoyable afternoon preparing for supper with Joe. Phyllis couldn't do much of the actual preparation, but she told Ellie what to do. And then she disappeared out into the garden. Ellie watched her go to the shed and come out with a trug. Intrigued, she edged nearer the door and observed through the window. With a determined look on her face, Phyllis bent towards a spring cabbage and hacked at it with a large knife. Ellie was on the point of going out to offer assistance, when the fresh green vegetable finally gave in to Phyllis's efforts. Then she moved on to another row where she plucked some spinach leaves. When the trug was half-full, she returned to the kitchen. Ellie saw her coming and ducked out of sight; she didn't want Phyllis to know she'd been watching her.

'Home-grown? I'm afraid I'll never make a gardener,' confessed Ellie.

'I can't dig now, but I saw a programme on the television about putting anything and everything in pots. They also gave advice about planning a raised bed. Joe came over and constructed it for me. There should be some strawberries later in the year.'

'Right, time for coffee, I think,' said Ellie, putting the finishing touches to the cottage pie, and laying the chopped vegetables to one side for cooking later.

'It's been a good day so far,' said Phyllis, sinking into her chair. 'Thank you, Ellie. I'm glad I got out with Ludo. And we've an exciting evening ahead of us.' She sipped her coffee and then dozed off. Ellie used the time to pop upstairs and see what she could wear. While it wasn't a proper date with Joe, she didn't want to slum it in the fashion stakes. She definitely wanted to make a good impression. If only she'd known she might meet a gorgeous man while here in East Anglia, she would have packed some more glamorous clothes. At least she'd packed some sensational shoes.

Joe arrived dead on half past six. Phyllis let him in and he made a fuss of Ludo.

'Can I get anyone a drink?' Ellie came down the stairs, hoping she wouldn't trip up in her high heels. She hadn't worn anything like that for ages and couldn't for the life of her remember why she'd included them in her luggage, although now she was pleased she had. They seemed to be serving a purpose, as Joe was looking her up and down, a slow smile creeping from his mouth to his eyes.

She felt a bit awkward and hurried into the kitchen to open the wine Phyllis had shown her earlier. Joe followed and watched as she fumbled with the corkscrew.

'May I?'

'No, it's fine. I think I can open a bottle of wine.' And with that the cork crumbled as she tried to pull it out of the bottle. 'Or maybe not.'

Joe took the bottle and blew the dust

off the label. 'It's a fine wine, but I have a feeling Phyllis stored it standing up and the cork has dried out. It's no surprise it crumbled. Shall I see what I can do?'

'Yes, please. I'll put the vegetables on to steam.'

After prising out the remaining cork, Joe filled the three glasses and carried them into the sitting room where Phyllis was waiting. 'To a speedy recovery,' he said, raising his glass.

'Not too speedy,' Phyllis said, looking pointedly at Joe. 'We want Ellie to stay for a little longer, don't we?'

'I've only got a week's holiday, so I hope you'll be much better by the time I go.'

Ellie left the two of them chatting while she saw to the meal. She was pretty sure Joe would be a microwave ready-meal man and thought their main course would be well received.

He certainly tucked in and seemed to be enjoying the food. 'Mmm, the vegetables are just right, Ellie.'

Phyllis chuckled. 'Not for me. I like mine well done, not all this under-cooked stuff.'

'The cottage pie is good. Your usual recipe, Phyllis? With a splash of Worcester sauce and your special homemade stock?'

'You know I always have a supply in the freezer.'

'I'd like the recipe if you're prepared to give your secrets away.'

Ellie thought it rather odd that Joe was asking for a recipe for homemade stock. Surely he used cubes or granules if he ever cooked from scratch, which didn't seem likely.

'And Ellie's concocted something for pudding.'

Ellie's cheesecake wasn't quite the success she'd hoped it would be, but then she couldn't imagine Joe ever bothering to make a pudding. He'd probably just serve ice-cream if he ever invited people for dinner. When she cut and served it, the pieces of cheesecake fell into a runny mess.

'I'm sure it will taste nice,' Joe encouraged.

'It's very good, dear,' Phyllis said. 'But probably not something you'll be serving in your restaurant, Joe.'

'Restaurant? What restaurant?' Ellie was horrified. Why hadn't Phyllis told her?

'I'm opening one on the seafront with the most fantastic view of the sea. I'm having some building work done at the moment so I'm managing Dad's shop while he and Mum are away on a cruise.'

'You mean you can cook?'

'He's done all the courses, dear, and he was the star pupil. And he's worked in a Michelin-starred restaurant.'

'Hold on, Phyllis, I wasn't the chef there.'

'As good as.'

Ellie slumped in her chair. She'd made all the wrong assumptions and felt a fool. They should have served something more adventurous. Something like flambéed chicken with

36

asparagus or salmon coulibiac which she'd seen in a magazine, not humble cottage pie, even if it was Phyllis's favourite. What would he think of her? But then again, why should she care? The answer to that was obvious.

'What's that?' Joe cocked his head to one side. 'That noise?'

'Ludo hasn't heard anything.' Ellie looked at the dog, who was curled up under the table.

'I told you he is rather deaf. But what can you hear, Joe?'

'Nothing now. I'm not sure what it was. Maybe a fox moving around. It sounded like scurrying. I thought there was something in the garden.'

'Not to worry. I expect it's the wind, or a fox as you said. Shall we have coffee now, Ellie?'

As Ellie put the instant granules into three mugs, she wished Phyllis had a coffee machine and could offer a choice of drinks. Even a cafetiere would be better than nothing.

She was subdued until Joe stood up

and offered to do the washing up.

'It's okay, we'll soon get that done when you've gone.'

'I was rather hoping you might come with me. Would you like to meet some of the locals? We could have a walk to the pub. It's got a good atmosphere. I think you'll like it.'

Ellie looked across at Phyllis. The thought of spending time alone with Joe appealed, but she was here for a purpose. She hoped Phyllis would agree to her going out with Joe.

'I'll be fine; you two young ones go off and have some fun. I'll read my book.' Phyllis settled back in her chair and waved them off with a dismissive hand.

Ellie felt uncomfortable as they set off down the path.

'Is something up, Ellie? You've been a bit quiet.'

'I just wish I'd known you are this super chef with Michelin stars.'

He put his hand on her arm. 'I'm not. I'm just an ordinary guy who likes to have meals with my friends. Phyllis's cottage pie is one of my favourites. I enjoyed the food, but more than that I enjoyed the company.'

Ellie's heart lurched a little. He seemed so nice. She wasn't looking for a relationship, but it would be good to spend a bit of her holiday with another young person.

The walk to the pub wasn't far and Joe pointed out places of interest along the way. 'That's the best place to go if you want a coffee,' he said, indicating a small café. 'It's cosy and the cakes are delicious.'

'Do you bake for them?'

Joe let out a roar of laughter. 'No, but it's a good idea. I'll have to add that to my business plan. Come on, Ellie, don't hold it against me that I do a bit of cooking.'

She grinned at him. 'I don't. I feel really silly that I thought I could impress you with my meal. Well, Phyllis was very helpful with telling me what to do.'

He shrugged and pulled her arm through his. 'I was just pleased to be invited. It was a treat for me. Okay?'

Ellie enjoyed the feel of her arm through Joe's and wished the walk to the pub was longer than it turned out to be. He released her and held open the door when they reached the Crown.

'Long time no see,' called the man behind the bar. 'You haven't been in for at least two days.'

Joe lifted a hand in salute. 'I was delivering stuff for the kitchen.'

'No need to explain to me,' said Ellie. 'I don't suppose there's a lot else to do in the town, is there? Besides coming in here or another pub for a drink and to socialise.'

'People here prefer a quiet way of life. There is a cinema and the pubs have snooker tables and this one runs bingo once a week. There was talk of an amusement arcade. Not many people were in favour of that, though.' He gestured for Ellie to sit down and then asked what she'd like to drink.

'Red wine, please. Better not mix my drinks. That bottle Phyllis had tasted really smooth. Is she a connoisseur?'

'Sort of. That is, she used to be. She's still got a few good bottles and can tell you something fascinating about each one. Mind you, if you listen to her stories, she appears to have been interested in a great many things.'

'I suppose you can't reach her age without knowing a thing or two. How old is she, any idea?'

Joe scratched his head and frowned. 'Around eighty, I suppose. She does well, or she did until this fall. It seems to have knocked the stuffing out of her. I thought she was quite subdued.' He went off to the bar and returned with the drinks.

'Tell me a bit more about the town, Joe. People seem friendly, or is that only to the locals?'

Ellie was disconcerted to find Joe wasn't paying her much attention. He was staring behind her in a distracted manner. When she turned to see what he was looking at, Joe said sharply, 'Don't look. Please, Ellie.'

Abruptly, she turned her attention back to him and decided to divert him. But the look on his face caused her words to stick in her throat. She was dying to look behind her and find out what was going on.

3

'I didn't mean to be rude,' apologised Joe a few minutes later. 'Someone I know is sitting behind you and I was surprised to see her, that's all.'

Ellie wasn't sure she liked the sound of that. Silly, she scolded herself, of course an attractive young man like Joe would have women friends. Or she could be someone as old as Phyllis. The idea of Joe being pursued by all the female pensioners in Fairsands made her giggle.

'What? What's funny?' Joe raised his eyebrows, a smile on his lips.

'Nothing,' she said. 'I was only thinking.'

Joe stood up.

'Are we going?' Ellie was surprised as they'd only been in the pub for a short time and hadn't even started a conversation.

Joe nodded, drained his glass and waited for Ellie to do the same. On the way out, they passed the table where Joe had seen the person he knew. He said, 'How are you, Amber?' Then, not even waiting for a reply, he ushered Ellie out of the door.

'What's happened to your friend?'

'No idea. I wouldn't call her my friend exactly.'

'Her face was grazed.'

'Was it? Come on, Ellie, let's walk back to Phyllis's.'

They didn't talk on the walk back and he didn't take hold of her arm. Once at Phyllis's gate he said, 'Goodbye, Ellie. Thank you for the meal. We must do something again some time.'

Ellie felt disappointed, but put on a smile when she found Phyllis in the sitting room. 'I didn't expect you to be up.'

'I wanted to make sure you got home safely.'

'I'm a big girl. My flatmates don't stay up for me when I go out.' Ellie giggled at the thought of them doing such a thing.

'It's just . . . ' Phyllis was trembling.

Ellie darted across and took her hand. 'What? What is it?'

'As you were leaving I heard a crash in the garden. It was as though someone was there.'

'It would be that fox Joe heard earlier. I'll check everything is locked up and then we'll go to bed. A good night's sleep will soon sort us out.' She hoped she sounded confident and had reassured Phyllis, but there was something disturbing Ellie, something in her subconscious she couldn't quite grasp.

The following morning Ellie was woken by the sun streaming through the gap in the curtains. She leapt out of bed and pulled them back. But gazing down into the garden she was aghast to see one of Phyllis's garden pots overturned and broken. Mud was strewn across the paving near the house and the plants lay withered.

She hurried downstairs in her dressing gown and rushed outside to clear it up. Just as she'd swept up the last of the mud, Phyllis appeared.

'I knew it. It wasn't a fox, was it? There was someone in the garden. There has been a spate of burglaries recently so I'd better report this to the police. Tommy will be round in no time. He usually enjoys my fruit cake, but he'll be disappointed today.' The chuckle that followed pleased Ellie. 'Now come along, let me make that phone call while you cook us some breakfast.'

Just as they were finishing scrambled eggs on toast there was a knock on the back door.

'It's only me, Tommy. I thought I'd better pop round and see the scene of the crime. How's that arm of yours? And who's this?'

Ellie took an immediate liking to Tommy, who had an easy, friendly way about him. Just how she imagined a local bobby should be.

'Ellie. She's helping me out for a week.'

'Nice to meet you.' He had an open face, round red cheeks and an infectious smile. 'I thought you'd like to know the London gang which has been targeting Fairsands and stealing from us has been caught. Just two days ago in fact. It will be in the weekly local paper so you'll be able to read all about it. They definitely aren't the culprits in this case. Will you show me?'

Ellie took the policeman into the garden and explained about the previous evening and what she'd found that morning.

'Mmm, certainly not a fox. It wouldn't have been able to knock such a heavy pot over. There are no footprints.'

Ellie felt awkward, as she'd swept up any evidence. 'Sorry.'

'It's all right. I understand you wanted to clear up so as not to upset Phyllis. I doubt there'd be anything anyway. It's a bit puzzling. Phyllis is

47

very popular in the town and I can't think who would be spying on her.'

'Spying on her! What do you mean?'

'Well they weren't here to steal her spring cabbages. What other explanation is there?'

'I don't know. If you've finished out here let's go back inside and I'll make a drink.'

If it wasn't for the worry of the stranger in the garden, Ellie would have enjoyed the chat between Tommy and Phyllis, who seemed to know each other well. The acerbic woman she'd first met had completely disappeared.

'Another item you'll be able to read about in the paper is the battle with that coffee chain. It seems the locals have won and planning permission won't be granted. The High Street will remain as it is, for now at least,' Tommy said with a satisfied smile.

'That's marvellous news. All that placard waving, handing out leaflets and getting the petition signed has been worth it. I wish someone had told me that we'd won.'

'I think everyone thinks you should be left in peace for a bit.'

'Not at all. You know I like to be in the thick of local goings-on. When did you hear?'

'This morning, as it happens. It was only public knowledge then.'

'I'm afraid I got you here under false pretences. I haven't been able to bake any cakes, but when I do, you'll have an extra-large slice or two.'

Ellie thought Fairsands was a livelier place than she'd imagined and there definitely seemed to be a community spirit. But she had two little niggles. One was the stranger in the garden, as she now thought of the incident, and the other was Joe's abrupt departure from the pub the previous evening.

'It's wonderful that Vanessa Good-john will be able to continue running her café in the High Street without competition from that chain.' Phyllis looked satisfied.

'I couldn't agree more. That's one of my favourite tea spots, along with this one. Here's to keeping Fairsands as a traditional seaside resort.' Tommy lifted his mug to toast the town.

★　★　★

After Tommy had left, Phyllis said, 'I think you ought to get some shopping. Will you nip down to Joe's? And then we can take Ludo for a little walk. I feel quite energetic after all that wonderful news.'

'Do we really need anything? Isn't there a supermarket? It would probably be cheaper. I could do a big shop rather than going down to Joe's all the time.' Ellie felt traitorous. She knew Phyllis would never do a big weekly shop at the supermarket when there was a selection of independent shops available. But Ellie didn't want to face Joe today after his unusual behaviour in the pub. She had an unwelcome feeling in the pit of her tummy that he might not have enjoyed her company.

'What on earth is it, Ellie? I thought you and Joe got on well. Did something happen last night?'

'No, nothing happened, except Joe decided to end the evening rather hurriedly. I hardly had time to finish my drink before he whisked me out of the pub and home.'

'How strange. I wonder why. That sounds very unlike the Joe I know. What an odd effect you've had on him, dear.'

Ellie decided to ignore Phyllis's comments, for the moment at least. 'Do you really want shopping, or is that an excuse to get me and Joe together?' She watched as Phyllis's cheeks pinkened.

A slow smile lit Phyllis's face. 'A bit of both if I'm honest. I felt I'd let Tommy down not having any cake to offer him. *I* can't bake, but *you* can.'

'Oh no I can't,' retorted Ellie. 'You saw what a mess I made of the cheesecake yesterday. There's no way I'm going to have my lack of cooking skills circulating the town, Phyllis

Dewar.' Ellie scowled, hoping she'd put her off.

'I'll show you how,' encouraged Phyllis. 'But we've run out of eggs. You scrambled the last of them for breakfast — and delicious they were, too.'

Ellie gave it some thought. It would be something to take both their minds off the recent events. 'Okay,' she agreed. 'Ludo could do with a walk. We can take the car and go along the seafront. What do you say?'

Phyllis nodded her head. 'I think I'd like that. I'd rather not be alone in the house at the moment.'

★   ★   ★

'Good morning, ladies,' said Joe. 'Have a seat, Phyllis. How are you feeling today?'

'All the better for seeing you.' Ellie could tell Phyllis was making an effort for Joe. She waited to see if she would tell him about the stranger in the garden incident. 'Tommy came round,' she said after a moment of silence.

'Social call, was it? To tell you about the coffee shop chain being vetoed?'

'Yes, that and to investigate an act of vandalism in my back garden.' Phyllis gripped the counter with her good hand. 'I didn't have any cake to offer him.'

To Ellie's dismay, tears appeared in Phyllis's eyes. She moved closer and put her arm around her. 'It's all right, Phyllis. The incident was enough to unnerve anyone. And you're still probably a bit in shock after your fall.'

Joe was by Phyllis's side in seconds. He squatted next to her. 'Poor Phyllis. You've been through a lot, haven't you? What happened in your back garden?' He listened intently as Phyllis explained about the invasion of her property and the broken plant pot. Gently he patted her shoulder. 'You've got a lot of friends around the town and now you've got Ellie to look after you.' He looked up at Ellie and the warm smile he gave her reached his eyes, making them sparkle like jewels.

Phyllis sniffed. 'I'm a silly old fool,' she admitted. She let out a shaky breath. 'We need eggs, Joe, and then we're taking Ludo along the seafront.'

'Wish I could come with you.' He took a carton of eggs from the cold shelf and rang up the amount on the till. 'You could have telephoned and I would have brought them over.'

'Ellie couldn't wait to see you,' said Phyllis, hardly suppressing a grin as she stood up and walked to the door of the shop.

As she started to protest, Ellie could think of nothing to say which would not make the situation worse.

'Would you like to go to the coffee shop with me, Ellie? Our one, I mean — the one the giants were trying to take over. We passed it last night.' Joe raised his eyebrows and waited.

'That would be lovely,' said Ellie. Then she lowered her voice. 'Phyllis is a bit distraught about the fact that someone's been in her garden. I can't leave her on her own. Anyway, after last night, I'm surprised you want to go anywhere with me.'

'Ah, yes, I'm sorry. I was preoccupied. I was rude and I apologise. Shall I drop by the house later, then? Perhaps I can help with putting things straight in the garden.' A couple of customers entering the shop took his attention. 'I'll bring you both up to date with the coffee shop details and my restaurant progress.'

He took Ellie's hand and squeezed it. So they were friends after all.

*   *   *

Phyllis was in the sitting room watching television with Ludo at her feet, and Ellie was in the kitchen admiring the fruitcake she'd made under Phyllis's instruction. She'd been told it improved on keeping, but was sure it wouldn't last long enough to find out.

The phone ringing took her attention

away from the cake. 'Shall I answer it, Phyllis? Probably a double-glazing salesman.' She lifted the receiver. 'Hello? Hello?' That was strange. No one replied. Not more peculiar goings-on, she hoped. 'Hello? Who's calling? Oh, hello, Susan. I thought you were a phantom phone caller. Yes, just a moment, I'll put her on.' She took the cordless phone to Phyllis. 'It's Susan. Her mum wants to speak to you.'

'Hello, dear. I didn't expect to hear from you when you're on holiday. Is it as good as you hoped? Have you met Mickey Mouse?' Phyllis chuckled and paused to listen to the reply. 'We're very well, thank you. Ellie has just made a wonderful cake *and* she's getting to know the locals. Joe's been round a few times. Oh, no, dear, that was all over a long time ago.'

Ellie didn't know what she was talk-ing about, but it was none of her business so she went back to the kitchen and wondered whether to attempt some more baking or not. No, she didn't want to spoil things for herself and have a disaster after her recent success. She'd go upstairs and tidy her room, then they could have a drink and slice of the delicious-looking cake. She gave it one more admiring glance before making her way upstairs.

★ ★ ★

'Are you ready for a cup of coffee, Phyllis?'

'That would be lovely. I was just thinking I'd try and make one, but then I heard you in the kitchen so thought I'd leave you to it.'

'I was upstairs. Perhaps it was Ludo you heard.'

Phyllis looked down at the carpet. 'I don't think so. He's been keeping my feet warm all afternoon.'

Ellie went into the kitchen and was horrified to see her beautiful cake smashed into pieces on the floor. Ludo had followed her and quickly began hoovering up the pieces, his tail wagging. 'No, Ludo, no. I have a feeling dogs aren't meant to eat cake.' She caught hold of his collar and took him back into the sitting room. 'I'm sorry Phyllis, there's been a disaster. Sit, Ludo.' The dog reluctantly did as he was told.

'What is it? You look pale.' Phyllis looked distressed.

'I can't understand what's happened. The cake is smashed on the floor. It can't have fallen off the table.'

'I said I heard someone in the kitchen. There's something very funny going on. We're going to have to keep the doors locked, even when we're here. I don't like it, I don't like it at all.'

'It does seem as though someone is out to scare us. We'd better call Tommy again. And this time I'll leave things as they are until he's been. We must keep Ludo out of the kitchen. I'll phone the police station now.'

'Oh, dear, oh, dear. We can't ask Tommy round. We've no cake to offer him!'

Ellie was pleased Phyllis was more concerned about entertaining the police constable than about the intruder in the kitchen, but was determined to report what had happened.

A knock at the back door alerted them to the arrival of another visitor. Ellie went to see who it was. 'Joe! Careful, don't walk in the cake. Come through. Phyllis and I have something to tell you.'

At the end of their tale Joe looked troubled. 'I haven't heard of anything else like this going on in the town, and in the corner shop we hear all the news and gossip. I don't want to worry you, but it seems to me you are being targeted for some reason. Do you know of anyone who might hold some sort of a grudge against you?' He looked at each of them in turn.

'Only that coffee shop chain. I was one of the leading lights in the protest. Do you remember, Joe? All those heated meetings.' Phyllis sounded proud. 'I expect the chain uses all sorts

59

of tactics to get their way.'

Ellie giggled. 'They're hardly going to send someone round to your house to smash your cake. It has to be something more personal. I'm sorry Phyllis, but it can't be anything to do with me. I've only been here for two minutes and I don't know anyone except you, Tommy and Joe. You haven't fallen out with any of your neighbours over anything, have you?'

'Don't be ridiculous. I don't have any enemies as far as I know. Maybe it's a youngster with nothing better to do than play practical jokes. You're the one with enemies, Joe.'

Joe laughed. 'You have a good imagination. But the point is, even if I did have, they wouldn't be getting at me by breaking your plant pot and spoiling your cake.'

'What's all this about?' Ellie asked. 'What's been going on?'

'Nothing, and it's all in the past now. It was all to do with where I'm opening the restaurant. It was a run-down building in a prime seafront position. The council wanted proposals as to how to use it. I put in my restaurant idea and someone else wanted to open an amusement arcade. It would have changed the whole character of the place. The opposition fought pretty hard . . . '

Phyllis interrupted, 'It even got as far as an attempt to bribe some of the councillors.'

'It's true, but with the backing of the local people my plan went through and I was allowed to rent the property. The idea of an unpretentious restaurant using locally sourced products went down very well with the locals. Most people were adamant that an amusement arcade wouldn't fit in with the sort of seaside town Fairsands is known as and loved for.'

Ellie admired his passion for his hometown. Was there anything she disliked about him? she asked herself. So far, she could think of nothing except his strange behaviour at the pub, which seemed completely out of character.

'It's impossible that the amusement arcade has anything to do with what's been going on here. We should report the incident and you must lock your doors.' Joe pulled his phone from his pocket and was soon deep in conservation with Tommy. Ellie secretly studied Joe. He was wearing a white T-shirt and fitted jeans. With his broad shoulders and strong muscles, not to mention his dazzling good looks, she thought he could be a model.

'Right, Tommy's on his way.'

Tommy arrived with an anxious look on his face. 'Phyllis, I'm sorry you've had these episodes of damage to your property.'

'I hope you find out who's doing it, Tommy. We've been wondering if someone is getting at me because of the coffee shop protest, but Ellie doesn't think that would be likely.' Phyllis put her hand down to stroke Ludo as if drawing strength from the animal.

Ellie's heart went out to the older lady who was trying so hard to be brave.

'We'll find them, Phyllis, don't you worry about that. But you must lock your doors at all times, and telephone the emergency services if it happens again. Not that it will,' Tommy added hastily.

'Joe's already told me to do that.' Phyllis sat upright and Ellie noticed a mischievous glint in her eyes. 'It's all your fault, Tommy.'

Tommy's red cheeks grew redder. 'Me? How am I to blame?'

'Ellie made you a cake and someone else took a fancy to it.'

They all laughed at Phyllis's attempt at making the situation better, and the atmosphere in the room lightened.

While Tommy continued his investigations, Joe suggested that he take Ellie and Phyllis to the coffee shop in town. 'We could do with a drink and there's no way Tommy will let us into the kitchen for quite a while. Besides, I've something to tell you.'

'We'll go in the car,' said Ellie, not wanting to put Phyllis under any more pressure. 'What about Ludo? Can we take him?'

Phyllis looked doubtful. 'He could stay in the car, but I'm sure he'll be fine in the sitting room with the door shut so he doesn't get in Tommy's way.'

★   ★   ★

'What a delightful place,' exclaimed Ellie as she helped Phyllis into the small café. Tables with pretty cloths were set higgledy-piggledy to make the most of the space available. Small vases of fresh wild flowers decorated each one.

'Now you can see why we didn't need a coffee chain. We're more than satisfied with what we've got here. Although there's not always a lot of room.' Joe acknowledged a few people.

Someone wearing a smart uniform topped with a starched white apron came over to them. 'Phyllis, how are you now? Poor you. We were all sorry to hear you'd been in the wars. Come on, I've got just the table.' She ushered them to a corner by the window. 'I'll bring a menu, but you know our range.'

'Should do by now, Vanessa. I'll have a large cappuccino and a vanilla slice.'

Ellie said she'd have the same and Joe ordered coffee and a raspberry Danish pastry. When they were sipping and nibbling, Ellie said, 'Joe, you were on the point of telling us something.'

Swallowing a piece of pastry, Joe grinned and said, 'How would you like to visit the pub again? There's a particularly good singer booked there this evening.'

'Okay, that would be nice. I like music,' said Ellie. 'What do you say, Phyllis?'

'What I say is that I would want to know who the person singing is.' Ellie didn't miss the wink from Phyllis to Joe and wondered what that was all about.

'His name's Joe Baines and he's got a wonderful voice. You'll love him, Ellie.' Joe grinned at her.

She thought about it. The name of Baines rang a bell, but she couldn't place from where. Then it hit her: Joe's parents' shop was called Baines Corner Store. 'It's you, isn't it?' When she received an answering grin from Joe, she said, 'Well, okay, I won't let that put me off. I'll come.'

'I think you've met your match there, Joe.' Phyllis lifted her cup to her lips and slurped at the frothy coffee.

'I hope so,' replied Joe, his smiling eyes glancing directly at Ellie. She could feel her cheeks growing hot and looked away.

They finished their snack and Joe went to the counter to pay.

'I'll just have a word with Vanessa if you don't mind, Ellie.' Phyllis hauled herself up from the chair and went over to Vanessa.

Not wanting to take up a table while she waited, Ellie walked over to Joe. 'I hope it won't be too much for Phyllis going out tonight.'

'She can't stay home on her own,

Ellie,' said Joe. 'It might do her good to have her mind taken off things.'

Back at the house, Tommy was just about to vacate the premises as he put it. His parting shot was, 'Take care, Phyllis. You too, Ellie. Don't take any chances.'

Having seen Tommy out, Phyllis said, 'Thank you both, I enjoyed that. It was nice to see Vanessa again and visit the café. By the way, I'm sorry to disappoint you, but Vanessa's coming round this evening to get me up to date with everything, so I won't be able to come to the pub. I expect you'll manage without me as a chaperone.' Then she went into the sitting room, leaving Ellie and Joe in the hallway.

Joe gripped Ellie's hand. 'I'm very fond of Phyllis, but I can't deny that I'll enjoy having you to myself this evening.'

Ellie felt a warm glow spread through her. She was looking forward to finding out more about Joe Baines.

4

After the coffee and cakes, neither Ellie nor Phyllis was very hungry, so Ellie prepared some sandwiches for their evening meal. 'What shall I put out for you and Vanessa to have later?' Ellie didn't like to snoop too closely in Phyllis's freezer or cupboards without being asked.

'There should be some biscuits somewhere. Is there a tin on the shelf above the fridge?'

'Got it,' called Ellie. She filled the kettle and put out mugs. 'I'd better go and change. Hope I've got something suitable for listening to a megastar.'

'I think you'll be impressed,' said Phyllis. 'Everyone loves Joe around here. Almost everyone.'

'Phyllis, you hinted at that earlier. Are you going to tell me what it's about?' Ellie was exasperated that Phyllis was keeping secrets; she was also

a bit wary as to what they might be.
'You ask Joe.'

* * *

'Wow, you look sensational.' Joe stood back and looked at Ellie. She was pleased she'd made a big effort to look good. The high-heeled shoes would be regretted if she had to walk far in them, but they were all right the other day on the way to the pub and back. The turquoise top was a favourite and she'd teamed it with black trousers. For once her hair had behaved itself and the quirky bob shone.

They'd make a good couple, decided Ellie as she looked at Joe. He wore a periwinkle blue shirt which brought out the colour of his eyes.

The pub was crowded when they walked in and Joe was greeted by a lot of people with much hand-shaking and back-slapping. 'I'll get the drinks. Do you want to find a seat?'

Ellie looked around for spare seats

and saw a table in the corner with just one person sitting at it. As she reached the table the woman turned and Ellie realised it was Amber who had been at the pub when Joe had acted so strangely. 'May we?' she asked.

'Yeah, sure.' Amber lifted her jacket from the chair beside her. Ellie smiled at her and sat down then looked for Joe. He was just leaving the bar and searching the crowd for her. She waved and he grinned and walked over. His smile disappeared as soon as he saw Amber.

'Hello, I'm surprised you're here tonight. I didn't think you were my biggest fan.'

'I like a laugh.' Amber smirked.

Joe leaned towards Ellie and said, 'I'm not sure these are very good seats. It's not close enough to the stage. Let's see what else we can find.'

Ellie looked around. The pub was jam-packed and there was nowhere else to sit as far as she could see. She didn't fancy standing, as her shoes had unexpectedly started to pinch. 'It's fine, Joe. Please sit down and give me my drink.'

Joe did as she suggested, but looked awkward. 'I'm going to have to go in a minute and tune up. Are you sure you'll be all right on your own? I wish Phyllis was here to keep you company.'

'You said you were pleased to have me to yourself earlier.'

Joe squirmed in his chair. 'Yes, but I won't be with you for most of the evening, will I? I didn't think of that. Shall I walk you back quickly? And you can have a nice chat with Phyllis and Vanessa.'

'No, Joe, I want to hear you sing. I can't wait. Go on, go and tune your guitar. Amber will keep me company.' She smiled at her companion.

Joe took his drink and disappeared into the crowd.

Ellie couldn't think how to start a conversation with Amber. She said the first thing that came into her head. 'Your face looks less sore than last time

71

I saw you. How did you hurt yourself?'

Amber quickly put her hand to her injury. 'It's nothing. I fell when I was out walking, that's all. The ground was rough.'

Ellie could tell she didn't want to talk about it so tried again. 'Are you local?'

'Yeah, I've lived here all my life. Me and Joe were at school together. He went off to college, but always came back to me. We've been going out for years.'

Ellie couldn't believe what she was hearing. Amber spoke as if they were currently together, although Joe had indicated he was hardly friends with her.

'We've broken up for a bit. He does that, Joe. Goes off with someone else for a while, but he always comes back to me. Always.' The way she said it was almost menacing.

'I see,' Ellie replied, but she didn't. Not that it was any of her business. She and Joe were only friends. It was all very odd. Joe hadn't seemed like the sort of man to jump from one relationship to another and then back again. Amber's revelation wasn't going to spoil her evening and she hoped to enjoy the music. 'What do you do?' she asked.

'I work in the supermarket, but as soon as Joe gets his restaurant going I'll be front of house. You know, greeting the customers, taking bookings, all that sort of thing.'

'That sounds interesting. I'm temping in an office. I should be there for a while. This is my holiday. I'm looking after . . . '

'I know — Phyllis. Everyone in the town thinks you're some sort of angel, coming here to look after a complete stranger. She's a right old nosey parker that Phyllis, her and her gang. Some of us wanted something lively going on here. An amusement arcade would have been fun for us young ones, but oh no, they don't want any changes.'

'I thought Joe's restaurant is opening

where the amusement arcade would have been.'

'Yeah, well, I could have got a job there. It would have been more exciting.'

Ellie's head was spinning. If she was Joe's girlfriend, surely she'd want the best for Joe. Instead she appeared not to care. The crowd started clapping and cheering and Joe appeared on the stage. Almost immediately he started to strum his guitar and sing. Ellie was stunned. He had the most beautiful voice and was singing one of her favourite Stevie Wonder songs. As he played the last chord the crowd roared.

'I'd no idea he would be so good.'

'I expect there's a lot you don't know about him. Listen, this one's our song.'

It was a love song and as Joe sang it he glanced across at their table. Ellie studied her hands knowing he was looking at Amber, not her.

The next number was more upbeat and several people danced in the small spaces between tables. Ellie realised this was her opportunity to make her escape and leave Joe and Amber to whatever was going on between them. If he was using her in some game to make Amber jealous she wanted nothing to do with it. Slipping out into the cool evening, she gave a huge sigh of relief. When she got back she would tell Phyllis she had a headache and go straight to her room.

* * *

''Morning, dear. I thought I smelt something cooking.'

'Will tomatoes with toast on the side do you for breakfast?' Ellie didn't want to be quizzed about the previous evening, but there was no way to prevent it.

'It was a shame about your headache.' Phyllis sorted out the cutlery they'd need. 'Isn't Joe a marvellous musician?'

'He is. Absolutely marvellous.' She knew her voice sounded dull.

'What is it? Do you still have a headache?'

'I'm fine. How was *your* evening?'

'It was fascinating. Vanessa has a lot of contacts, some of them through her husband. He works at the council, not in planning, but he knows what's going on. The developer who wanted to open an amusement arcade here has had his planning application turned down in a town further up the coast as well. He's furious.'

'Maybe they'll give up now.' She stopped what she was doing. 'I've just seen a movement in the garden.'

'Where?' Phyllis bobbed up to have a look out of the window. 'It's Joe. What's he doing?'

'I don't know.' She didn't like to add she didn't care. 'It looks as though he's planting up a new pot. Here's your breakfast. I'm going to my room for a lie down.'

'But I thought you said your head was better.'

Ellie didn't reply and was already on

her way to the stairs. She didn't like being abrupt with Phyllis, but she couldn't remain downstairs and possibly have to face Joe; it was more than she could bear. The events of the previous evening still played in her mind and caused her anguish.

Only a few more days to go and she could be out of Fairsands for good, thought Ellie as she sat on the edge of her bed. She'd tidied everything in sight and had even sorted her clothes into some kind of colour order. She was just biding her time until Joe left. Then she'd have to consider Phyllis. And Ludo. The poor creature would want a walk.

A quiet tap came at her bedroom door. Thinking it was Phyllis, she quickly opened it a crack. But it was Joe. He raked his fingers through his hair.

'What's wrong?' asked Ellie, hoping Phyllis was all right.

'Ellie, please talk to me. Phyllis said you were hiding up here, but . . . '

'I was *not* hiding,' insisted Ellie. 'Well, just for a while perhaps. What do you want to talk about?' Face to face with Joe, she felt a bit of a fool for having tried to escape. It would have been better if she'd stayed downstairs. She wondered what was so important that he had come to find her.

'Why you left without saying cheerio yesterday and why you're avoiding me now.' Joe took a step back and crossed his arms. 'Was my performance so awful you had to get away quickly last night?' He grinned at her and he was immediately transformed from a cranky person into the happy one Ellie had grown fond of. But, she reminded herself, he was off-limits to her; he was Amber's boyfriend.

'I think you've got a fantastic voice, but I got the impression that I was a bit of a gooseberry.' Ellie couldn't help it; she wanted to be nice to Joe, but she was disappointed at his less than honest explanation of his involvement with Amber.

Joe looked surprised. 'What do you mean? I've no idea what you're talking about. Amber said you just up and left without a word.'

Ellie replied, 'That's true. But she told me you and she were an item and I felt a bit awkward having walked into the pub with you when you were with her, if you see what I mean.'

Joe leant towards Ellie and put his hands lightly on her shoulders. 'Ellie, I swear to you that Amber and I are not together. We went to the same school, so we've known each other a long time. For some reason or other she's obsessed with me. We did go out for a while, but that was a long time ago and I finished it. She was too possessive and clingy. We weren't right for each other and I'm not in the slightest bit interested in her.' That speech took the wind out of Ellie's sails. Straightaway, she felt happier than she had in a long while. But Joe was still talking. 'When I was singing that Stevie Wonder number I was singing to you, Ellie. Although

I'm sorry Phyllis had a fall, I'm really pleased you came to Fairsands.' He moved his hands from Ellie's shoulders down her arms and clutched her wrists. 'So, are we friends again?' Ellie agreed and let herself be persuaded downstairs.

'Go and have a look at what Joe's done,' called Phyllis from the sitting room.

Together Ellie and Joe went out through the back door. 'You have been busy,' said Ellie. 'That hanging basket is really pretty and so are the plants in the container.'

'Let's hope that's where they'll stay. I don't want another episode of vandalism here. I wonder who's causing it and why.'

'Do you think Amber might have anything to do with it?' Ellie hated saying anything, but wanted to get the subject out of the way. She'd thought about it long and hard ever since detecting the sourness in her last night.

'Amber? No. She's not as gentle as

some people, but her heart's in the right place. She wouldn't want to harm Phyllis. What possible gain would there be?'

'I'm sure you're right.'

'I'd better be getting back. Jane, the assistant at the shop, will want to get off. I'll be bringing Ludo's food later in the week so if there are any items I can deliver at the same time, just let me know. Although I hope I'll see you before then.' He strode off.

Ellie marched into the sitting room and opened her mouth to speak, but Phyllis got there first. 'I know, I shouldn't have sent him up to your room, but I knew you wouldn't come down. It was obvious you'd had a falling out. Want to talk about it?' Phyllis raised her eyebrows.

'Not really,' replied Ellie. 'Anyway, we're friends again now.' She sat down on the settee and was pleased when Ludo shuffled over and rested his head on her foot. 'Phyllis, the days are going by quickly and I'll have to go home at the weekend. How are you going to manage? It's difficult to do things with one hand even when you're as resilient as you are.'

'I'll be all right. Of course, I might need help walking Ludo and carrying a bit of shopping, although Joe will deliver things if I ask him. Don't you worry about me.'

'But I do,' insisted Ellie. 'Especially with this vandalism business. I wonder who can be behind it.'

Phyllis shook her head. 'No idea, but it will probably stop now that Tommy's involved.' Ellie had her doubts that Tommy would deter anyone; he was so pleasant. 'Vanessa said she'd keep me company, but she's busy in the café and, of course, she's got her own family to look after. Now, I think it's time for Ludo's walk, don't you?'

This time they didn't head towards the seafront. Phyllis wanted to show Ellie the area around her home. They sauntered along the pretty streets and Phyllis chatted about the people she knew in the houses they passed. 'And that's where Amber lives,' stated Phyllis, taking Ellie by surprise. She had no idea she was that nearby. As they went by the house, Ellie caught sight of Amber behind the net curtains. And she was not looking at all happy.

5

'What's wrong with you, Ellie? The sun's shining, the garden's looking pretty and we're enjoying *another* of your delicious cakes.'

Ellie had to admit all the things Phyllis mentioned were good. They were sitting on the bench in the garden enjoying the morning sunshine. She was very pleased that her baking skills had progressed during the week under Phyllis's watchful eye. 'I just wish I wasn't going home tomorrow. For two reasons. I don't want to leave you to fend for yourself, and I've had a lovely time. Maybe I'm greedy, but I'd like it to last a bit longer.'

'And then there's the third reason. Joe.'

'I *do* like Joe, but we're friends, nothing more. He should be popping in soon so that we can work out the rota for walking Ludo and helping you out.'

'I'll make myself scarce when he comes, but please don't overdo the help. I want to get back to normal as soon as I can. Here he is now.'

The gate opened and Ellie brightened up on seeing Joe.

'Come on, dear. Ellie's made lemon drizzle cake today. It's delicious. You can sit here. I'm off inside for a little nap.'

'I'll go and make a pot of tea.' Ellie made to stand, but Joe grabbed her hand to stop her.

'No, don't go. Let's not waste any of the time we can spend together. I'm going to miss you when you go back, Ellie. Will you visit? Soon?'

'I'd like to. Do you think Phyllis would put me up?'

'I'm sure of it. She's going to miss you too. In spite of her talk of independence, I think she needs a bit of support for a few more weeks. I've got some deliveries to make, so let's work out the rota, and then I can text people to tell them when they're on duty.'

'Who have we got? There's Vanessa, but she can only do one or two evenings a week. Tommy said he and his wife want to be on the rota, and you said Jane would help.'

'And there's me and a couple of the neighbours, including Amber.'

'Amber?'

'Why not? She's a neighbour and knows Phyllis.'

Ellie didn't feel comfortable with the thought of Amber looking after Phyllis, but she supposed she hardly knew her and was in no position to judge her caring abilities. 'How do you know she wants to help?'

'She came into the shop. She's got some tickets for an open-air concert with some really good bands and asked me to go with her.'

'That's nice.' It was just as well she was leaving tomorrow. She could get back to normality with no handsome man tugging at her heartstrings. 'I've got a piece of paper so if I divide it into the days of the week and divide each day into morning, afternoon and evening, we can put a name in each section.' Ellie enjoyed Joe's closeness as they worked out the rota of Phyllis's helpers.

'There, that's good. All we need to do is tell people when they're needed.'

After Joe had let people know the schedule, he said, 'I wondered if you'd like me to cook a meal for you tonight. Dad's got a few good bottles of wine and he won't mind if we sample one. You'll have to come to my parents' house, but it's not far. I'm there temporarily until the flat above the restaurant is ready for me to move into. If you don't want to drive, I could come and fetch you or you could use Phyllis's old bike. It's a really ancient sit-up-and-beg type, but does the job.'

'I can't.'

'What? Cycle?'

'Leave Phyllis, not on my last evening here.'

'All sorted.' Joe grinned. 'Jane's

agreed to come over this evening.'

'How presumptuous of you! But as I want to see if your cooking is all it's hyped up to be, I'd love to come.' She wasn't going to miss the opportunity of an evening with him, even though she felt there was more to Joe and Amber than she knew. 'I'll spend the whole afternoon with Phyllis and Ludo. We might have an outing to give her a change of scene.'

'You're so lovely, Ellie. Are you sure there's no way you could stay a bit longer?' He took her hand and she let him hold it.

'I don't want to lose my job.' She jumped up. 'That's Phyllis's phone ringing. I'd better go and answer it. Text me the address and time.' Ellie bounded indoors. 'It's all right, Phyllis; I've got the phone. I'll bring it through. It's Susan's mother, Diane.' Ellie took the cordless phone through to the sitting room and handed it over. Phyllis waved for her to sit down.

'I'm absolutely fine, thank you. Well,

that's true, she is going home tomorrow, but they've sorted a rota for people to take Ludo out, just while I recover fully.'

Ellie smiled at the way Phyllis didn't want anyone to think she was dependent on her friends and neighbours.

'Really, I don't need mollycoddling. You get back to work. Now let's change the subject. Tell me all about Paris.' She paused to listen. When she'd finished the call she handed the receiver back to Ellie. 'What a fuss and bother. She wants to come down here and look after me. Ridiculous.'

'She's anxious about you, Phyllis. Don't worry, I'll be seeing Susan at work next week and I'll reassure her that you can manage.'

* * *

Ellie found Joe's parents' house easily following the instructions he'd given her. It felt good to be on a bike again. The only exercise she'd had was walking with Phyllis and Ludo, and neither of them went far or fast. She reflected that, once home, she'd have to get back into her routine of jogging and cycling. Too much cake and cooked breakfasts had made her waistband tight.

'Come in, Ellie,' invited Joe. 'I'll put your bike through the side gate. Not too puffed out, are you?'

'Of course not.' Ellie tried to slow her breathing to a normal rate. She didn't want Joe thinking she was unfit.

'Go straight through and I'll be with you in a minute.'

Ellie wandered along the hallway looking at the photos on the wall. She paused as she came to one of a rascally-looking young boy and grinned widely as she recognised Joe. He was handsome even as a lad. She moved on as Joe banged the front door shut.

'Through there,' he said.

'What a beautiful room, and the table's lovely.' Ellie looked around admiringly.

'All part of the service,' said Joe. 'Seriously, I do think it's important to create an inviting atmosphere as well as providing tasty food. But I hope you're not expecting anything fancy.'

'You mean we've got beans on toast?' she quipped.

Joe laughed. 'You know, I don't think you'd mind if I did produce that, would you?'

Ellie shook her head. She wouldn't mind anything now she was in Joe's company. She had never felt so relaxed and comfortable with a man before. Previous boyfriends had been rather distant and tense and she wondered if she brought out the worst in them, but being with Joe felt just right. Only a few days ago she'd wanted the time to fly by so she could return home, but now she wanted to stay.

Joe popped out to the kitchen and returned with a bottle of wine. He filled two glasses and passed one to Ellie. 'To you,' he toasted her. 'And a wonderful evening ahead.'

'How's your restaurant coming along, Joe? You were going to take me to see it, but we never did get round to it.'

'Funny you should bring that up.' Joe frowned. 'I called in there to check on things earlier and there were scratch marks on the bar. No idea how they got there. It was fine the other day and the builder is adamant he hasn't been working anywhere near that area since I was there last. Anyway, he says he'll plane it down and give it another coat of varnish. Strange though.'

Immediately Ellie's thoughts ran to Amber. And then she felt ashamed of herself. But she wanted to be sure. 'Has anyone got a grudge against *you*, Joe?'

'Me? No, everyone loves me. At least that's what Phyllis keeps saying.' Joe chuckled. Ellie remembered that was what Phyllis had told her as well, although she'd also mentioned that Joe had enemies even though he'd laughed away the suggestion. 'Now come and sit at the table and let's enjoy the evening.'

The starter of seafood in a light cheese sauce wrapped in filo pastry was the most delicious thing Ellie had ever tasted, and she wasn't slow in telling Joe.

'Locally sourced. Glad you're enjoying it. I'm experimenting on you. I figured if you like it, then so would the customers.'

While Joe cleared the plates and put some finishing touches to the main course, Ellie had time to think. Why would anyone want to damage the restaurant? She decided to ask Joe when he returned.

With a plateful of chicken in white wine sauce with mashed potatoes and colourful carrots and peas in front of her, Ellie said, 'This looks delicious. You've definitely presented it well. It looks really pretty.'

'They say you eat with the eyes first, if you know what I mean. If it looks good then it usually tastes good.' Joe

93

sipped at his wine. 'This is a dish I want included on the restaurant menu as well.'

'Definitely. What a pity I don't live closer. I'd be a regular.'

Joe's hand rested on her arm. 'I'd hate for us not to see each other again. Fate is cruel to take you away before we've got properly acquainted.'

The look in his eyes had an unexpected effect on Ellie. Even though he'd said the words in a flippant way, there was no mistaking his meaning. She felt herself growing hot and it wasn't a result of the food. 'When will you be open for business?' she asked.

'Should only be a couple of weeks now. It's quite exciting, but I think a few people are angry that an amusement arcade was turned down in favour of the restaurant.'

Ellie thought of Amber, but didn't say anything. She didn't want Joe to think she was leading a hate campaign against the woman. 'I thought most people wanted a restaurant,' was all she said.

'Most people, yes. I know the property developer who wanted the space. He's often around the area nosing out land, but he doesn't have a lot of luck. You'd think he'd move on to pastures new. He's made it clear that he's not pleased with me. Anyway, enough of this talk. Tell me a bit more about yourself, Ellie.'

After another delicious course of fresh fruit salad with a chocolate coulis, Ellie sat back and surreptitiously undid the top button of her trousers. 'I can't eat anything else.'

'That's lucky. It's all I've got. I can make coffee later if you like. But no pressure. Shall we relax and listen to some music?' Joe left the plates on the table and put on a CD of ballads. He hummed along to the tunes. 'We could dance.'

'I think I should be going, Joe. I'm having a great time with you, but Jane won't want to be late home, especially if she's working at your shop in the morning. Will I see you again before I leave tomorrow?'

'Yes, you will,' promised Joe. 'I'll get your bike. Hope you don't wobble off.'

'Cheek!' Ellie chuckled.

It was a balmy, moonlit evening, just right for a bicycle ride. When Joe brought the bike round she kissed him on the cheek. 'Thanks, Joe. It's been a lovely evening.'

Joe leaned forward and she knew what would happen next if she let it, but it was going to be bad enough leaving the next day without thoughts of Joe's lips on hers. 'I'll see you.' She quickly hopped on the bike and sped off.

Cycling through the dark, she enjoyed the feel of the breeze on her cheeks, and as she sped along she began to feel more cheerful. As she approached the only sharp bend on her route home, she clutched the brakes. Nothing happened. She tried again. Nothing. She'd have to take the corner at speed and hope for the best.

'Ooh, ow,' she groaned as she lay in a heap on the ground with the bicycle on top of her. She pushed it off and rubbed her legs and knees. Gingerly, she pushed herself into a sitting position. Apart from the shock of the accident and a few scrapes, Ellie thought she was unscathed. She stood and set off for Phyllis's, pushing the bike along. It was an old bike, she knew that, but she'd ridden to Joe's with no problem. Something had happened while the bike was at Joe's, she was certain. Amber? Surely the woman wouldn't attempt to kill her, however strongly she felt for Joe. Relieved that she would be going back to her normal life tomorrow, she couldn't help worrying about her new friends and what might happen to them.

After putting the bike in the shed she went inside, hoping Phyllis wouldn't question her too closely.

'Hello, dear. Jane's just left. Nice

time?' Phyllis peered over the top of her glasses. 'Ellie! Whatever's happened to you?'

Ellie wasn't sure if she should tell the truth or not. She didn't want Phyllis worrying. 'I went too fast round a bend and lost control. I'm afraid the bike needs fixing. I'm sorry.' It wasn't the whole truth, but it wasn't a lie either.

'Don't worry, as long as you're not badly hurt.'

'I'm fine. How was your evening, Phyllis?'

'Very nice. Jane's good company. We'll ask her husband, Mick, to fix my bicycle. He's an experienced electrician, but is generally handy and good at things like that. Joe asked him to do the wiring for his place. Jane doesn't say much, but they're struggling financially. Although they're loyal to Joe, the amusement arcade would have been a much bigger contract and helped them out of a hole.'

As Ellie made bedtime drinks she couldn't help thinking that someone who could fix bikes could also damage them. Maybe Mick was trying to get at Joe. But why would he target her? No, it had to be Amber, because she didn't like Joe having another female friend.

★   ★   ★

After breakfast the following morning, Ellie packed and took her luggage to the car. Phyllis and Ludo stood on the doorstep.

'It was very kind of you to come and keep me company, dear. And I know Ludo's going to miss you.'

Ellie interpreted that to mean that Phyllis would miss her. She felt tearful at the thought of leaving. Despite a few misgivings, she had enjoyed her time by the sea. There was no sign of Joe, even though he'd said he'd see her before she left. When she could put off her departure no longer, she hugged Phyllis and bent down to stroke Ludo. 'I'll keep in touch,' she promised. 'And you take care of yourself, Phyllis. Goodbye.'

As she drove away, Ellie scanned the surrounding area for a sign of Joe. Where was he? He'd promised to come and see her off. She wondered what had happened to him.

6

Ellie had been sad to leave Fairsands, but was happy to be back at the flat and catch up with all the news. Sunday evening wasn't her favourite time, so she decided she'd have a long soak and prepare herself mentally for the following day when she'd be back at work. It would be good to see Susan and her other workmates again. She'd been there for a few months now so knew people quite well. Just as she was about to go to the bathroom, her phone alerted her to a message. Hoping Joe was getting in touch, she was surprised to see it was from her boss. She couldn't believe what she read. She was being given the push, and by text. A range of emotions ran through her. Her first thought was to phone Susan.

'I'd no idea. That's awful. They've been talking about making cuts, but they didn't say anything about getting rid of staff. What will you do?'

'What can I do? Look for another job. I'll have to go to the employment agency and see if they have anything else.'

'I'm really sorry you won't be at the office. We'll make arrangements to meet up and have a gossip, but I'll have to go now. The kids are supposed to be asleep and it sounds like a circus up there. I'll talk to you tomorrow.'

Ellie was disappointed. She needed to talk to someone about her future and her flatmates had gone out. Not knowing if it was the right thing to do, she phoned Joe and told him she'd been sacked.

'That's great!'

'No, it isn't. I haven't got a job.'

'You can come back here. I'm really happy. This has solved my problem.'

'That's all right then. So long as you've got what you want, Joe Baines.' Ellie was still upset that Joe hadn't bothered to come to wave her off when she left Fairsands.

'I'm sorry about your job, but it didn't sound as though you really enjoyed it. The thing is, I need to spend more time at the restaurant, and once it's open I won't have any time left for the shop. So if you managed the shop that would be perfect.'

'And what would Jane think about me waltzing in and taking charge?'

'She'll be fine. She likes you.'

Ellie kept her earlier thoughts of Mick and the bike to herself. 'And I suppose you'd expect Phyllis to put me up.'

'Not at all. Mum and Dad have a caravan on the seafront you can have. It's quite new and the site has all mod cons. It's what we think of as our family caravan. We just let relatives and friends use it.'

'You've got it all worked out then. I'll work in your shop and live in your caravan.'

'What do you think? Say yes, please. It's not about the shop, it's that I want to get to know you better. If you live here we can spend more time together. *And* you can join Phyllis's rota.'

'Can I think about it? I'll ring you back later.' Ellie's head was spinning. She'd gone from being made redundant to being needed in the space of a few minutes. Letting herself consider that it was Joe who wanted her sent her into a daydream. It would be good to spend more time with him. With the exception of Amber, the people she'd met at Fairsands had been pleasant and friendly. Could she make a long-term commitment to stay in East Anglia over the summer? When she heard her flatmates return, she went into the sitting room to join them.

'It seems I've lost my job with the agency,' she informed them. They were sympathetic.

'You'll get another job easily,' one assured her.

'It's not that simple.' Ellie realised she'd made up her mind what to do. 'I'm not sure I want to stay in this town. When I was in East Anglia I met someone who's looking for a manager for his shop. I've been offered the job.' She looked around and smiled at her friends. 'I've decided to accept. I'll be moving out as soon as I can pack my things. Of course, I'll pay the rent for the next couple of weeks so as not to leave you in the lurch.' Ellie desperately hoped her bank manager would be understanding.

'My cousin's looking for a room. She might like to move in,' said another of the flatmates. 'We'll be sorry to see you go, Ellie. Stay in touch, won't you?'

It had gone more easily than Ellie anticipated. She was free to do what she wanted. Did she want to live in a caravan in East Anglia? You betcha! 'Joe? I'm packing right now, but probably won't travel over until Tuesday.'

'You've no idea how happy that makes me, Ellie. Drive carefully.'

Ellie opened the car window and breathed in the fresh sea air. It was a beautiful day and she felt she'd come home. As she got out of the car, she stretched her arms in front of her and wanted to run along the seafront.

'Ellie. Great to see you.' Joe bounded out of the shop, much to the interest of his customers. 'Leave your stuff in the car for now. Let me finish serving and then I'll make some tea.'

In the little area behind the shop, Joe arranged two mugs and opened a packet of chocolate biscuits. 'Does Phyllis know you're here?'

'No. I could phone her, but I thought I'd call round later. I didn't want to interfere with the rota.'

'Jane's there at the moment. But she'll be leaving in about an hour to start her shift here. By the way, why didn't you tell me about your bicycle accident?'

'Did Phyllis let on?' Ellie had asked her not to say anything.

'No, Mick did. He said the brake

cables were dodgy.'

Ellie couldn't dismiss the idea that someone had tampered with the bike. Anxious to change the subject and hoping her decision to return to Fairsands hadn't been a foolish one, she said, 'I'm looking forward to seeing the caravan. I'd better buy some supplies before I go though. Bread, milk and other basics. I didn't ask how much the rent would be.' She'd only just thought of that. Of course, Joe's parents wouldn't let it out to her for nothing.

Joe looked surprised. 'There's no rent involved. You're doing me a favour. Plus there's a wage for looking after the shop. Make yourself comfortable, Ellie, and I'll take you through the deal stage by stage. We can't tell you exactly when you'll be starting. I need to fit you in around Jane and me so I'll have to look at our present rota and think about it.'

Relaxing in Joe's company, Ellie listened as he outlined her duties, hours and responsibilities. She was sure he was giving her preferential treatment, but she was in no position to argue. She just hoped she did the job justice and Joe's parents had a profitable business to return home to.

★　★　★

'This is the caravan,' said Joe, opening the door and standing aside for Ellie to go in. 'Not a lot of room, but it's got most things.'

'I didn't expect a television and microwave,' admitted Ellie, as she dumped her bags of groceries on the table. Everything seemed to have been thought of. It was a lovely cosy place and she knew she'd be happy living there. 'What's this? A wardrobe?' She opened a sliding door and revealed a small shower room. 'Gosh, things have improved since my caravanning days with Mum and Dad.'

'So you're happy with it?' Joe looked apprehensive. 'I thought you'd be a bit put off by it to be honest.'

'I love it,' Ellie assured him.

Joe let out a breath. 'Good.'

'I've never worked in a shop, you know,' said Ellie. 'And I haven't a clue how to operate the till.'

'There's time to teach you all of those things. I'm sure you'll pick things up easily. You're bright!' Joe gestured towards Ellie's car. 'I'll bring your luggage in and let you get settled. I'd better get back to the shop. The least I can do is take you out for a meal this evening. What do you say?'

'Yes, please,' said Ellie. 'When I'm sorted here I'll pop over and see Phyllis and Ludo. It's only been a couple of days, but I've kind of missed them.'

Joe bent to drop a kiss on the top of Ellie's head. 'See you about half seven.'

Ellie enjoyed setting out her things in her new home. She wondered what the neighbours were like.

Changing into her tracksuit, she decided to jog to Phyllis's house. It would be a good start to this new chapter of her life. And if Joe was taking her out to eat, she'd have to work off some calories beforehand.

★   ★   ★

'You can't get rid of me,' grinned Ellie as she followed Phyllis into her sitting room. 'Did Joe tell you I was coming back?'

'He hinted that there was a surprise in store.' Phyllis's eyes shone. 'I did wonder if you were involved, as he looked very pleased with himself. Sit down and tell me what's happening. I need something to interest me now that the commotion of the coffee chain has died down.'

Ellie brought her up to date and asked how the rota was working out.

'You and Joe did a good job between you. It's lovely having people popping in and out and I'm sure it won't be long before I'm doing everything myself again.'

Although she wasn't sure how true that was, Ellie wasn't going to dampen

Phyllis's spirit. Instead she said, 'I'll invite you to the caravan for tea — if you've some free time, that is.'

Phyllis bent towards Ellie. 'Between you and me, I'm not sure how keen Jane is.'

Puzzled, Ellie asked, 'On what?'

'Visiting me. She's been very pleasant and helpful, but she seems preoccupied. I think Ludo's noticed as well. He won't take any notice of her when she comes round now. They used to get on well. I don't think she'll take him out for a walk. But Tommy will, so that's all right, and his wife is a nice woman. You must meet her.'

'I'd better be getting back now, Phyllis. I'm meeting Joe later.'

'Hot date, is it?' The two women laughed.

$\star$　$\star$　$\star$

After a shower, Ellie brushed her hair and squirted on some perfume. She was excited at the thought of spending time with Joe. Maybe being sacked was the best thing that could have happened to her. A new life in a new place. When she heard the tap on the door her heart leapt.

'Hello. Wow, you look great! I hope you won't be disappointed in the place I'm taking you. You should be going to the Ritz.' He took both her hands. 'You can't imagine how pleased I am that you're back. I know it was horrible for you to lose your job and I'm sorry you've had to leave your friends and flatmates to come here. But for me it's perfect. And we're going to have a perfect evening together to celebrate your return. Shall we go? Is it all right if we walk? It's not far.'

As they walked along the seafront they chatted companionably together. 'Nearly there. Just round this corner. Ta dah!'

'Your restaurant? Is it open?' Ellie couldn't imagine that it was, as the outside needed a coat of paint and it didn't look at all like a good restaurant.

There was a pile of rubble outside and no sign giving the name of the place.

'It's open just for us. I'm so thrilled, and I wanted to share my excitement with you. The interior is finished. I want to show you everything and I want you to be the first person I cook for in my new restaurant.'

He led her inside through the back door and showed her round the kitchen, which was all shiny surfaces and state-of-the-art appliances. Then he proudly led her into the dining room with its cosy corners and gingham cloths.

'It's lovely. It reminds me of a French restaurant I went to once.'

'I wonder if that was the same one I've based this on! Let me show you to your table.' He led her to a table laid with its blue-checked cloth and a vase with a single red rose. After he had shaken out a napkin, placed it on Ellie's lap, and poured them each a glass of white wine, he disappeared to the kitchen. 'Seafood choux puffs,' he announced, putting a plate at each place.

'Mmmm, smells delicious. And it looks good too.' The taste matched up to her expectations and soon their plates were empty. 'Phyllis seemed in good spirits. She was very surprised to see me. Pleased too, I think. So was Ludo. I didn't like to ask Phyllis, but has anything odd happened while I've been away?'

'Nothing as far as I know.'

'I've been thinking about those strange incidents and wondering why someone would do such things.'

'We don't know that anybody has done anything. All that's happened is something broke a pot in Phyllis's garden and the brakes on your bike didn't work. Oh, yes, and your cake was smashed.'

'*All* that's happened. You may think I'm being dramatic, but I could have been killed. And you've forgotten that your bar was damaged as well.'

'I meant to let you know. My builder

told me his apprentice owned up to damaging the bar. It was an accident. Come on, Miss Marple, they could *all* have been accidents and totally unconnected. I know that in a place as quiet as Fairsands we have to make our own entertainment, but if you want a murder mystery weekend try the Old Hall. I'll fetch the main course. I think you'll like it.'

As Joe cleared away the empty plates, Ellie ran through the people she knew in Fairsands who might be a suspect. Top of her list was Amber. Then she considered Mick, and Vanessa's husband, who worked for the council. Mick would have been better off with the amusement arcade contract, and Ellie wondered if Vanessa's husband would have been one of those offered a bribe to get the amusement arcade plans passed. Now she was being silly.

Her thoughts were broken by shouts of, 'Ellie, Ellie, phone the fire brigade!' from Joe in the kitchen. He rushed back in. 'The kitchen's on fire!'

Ellie dialled 999 and handed the phone over. 'You speak to them. I don't know the address.'

Joe grabbed her hand and pulled her out of the building through the front door and across the street as he spoke into the phone. Within minutes a fire engine arrived.

Joe slumped against a wall. 'My dream, Ellie, up in smoke.'

'Oh, Joe, I'm sorry.' She hugged him to her. 'You can sort it out, I'm sure.'

'Possibly, but my budget's tight and there was a timescale I had to stick to.'

'You are insured?'

'Thank goodness.'

'Let's look on the bright side.'

Joe almost smiled. 'Trust you, Ellie. There's a crisis and you can find a bright side.'

'Yes, if we hadn't been at the restaurant you wouldn't have seen the fire and the whole place could have been ablaze before it was spotted.'

'That's true. It wasn't exactly how I hoped our evening would turn out, although I thought there might be a few sparks.' He gently stroked her cheek. 'I wonder what caused the fire.'

'Who's been working there today?'

'Several people. Mick was finishing off the electrics . . . '

'There's your answer.' In Ellie's mind a question formed. Was it an accident, or deliberate? And then another question came into her head. Had Joe told someone they were having a meal there? And if so, had the arsonist wanted to harm them?

'Are you the man who rang, sir?' The fireman took his helmet off.

'I'm the owner. How do things look to you?'

'Not too bad. There's quite a bit of smoke and water damage, of course. All quite superficial considering what might have happened. We'll be investigating the cause tomorrow and let you know our findings. We'll make sure the rest of the building is secure for the night. You need to get home and have a nice cup of tea or something stronger.'

'That's right. Come on Joe, let's go back to the caravan and I'll drive you home.' Ellie took his arm.

'Thank you, officer. I'm very grateful. Please pass on my thanks to everyone involved.'

As they walked back along the seafront, Ellie asked, 'What was it we were going to have for our main course?'

'Baked stuffed aubergines. It's a recipe I picked up in Turkey. I travelled round for a while and worked in restaurant kitchens in various countries.'

'There's a lot I don't know about you, Joe Baines. Why don't you come in and I'll make a cup of tea and some toast. I'd like to hear about your travels and it might take your mind off the fire.'

Despite his obvious shock and worry, Joe was very entertaining with his descriptions of the places he'd visited and the things he'd seen in some of the kitchens abroad. He drained the last of his tea and ran his hands through his hair. 'I'd best be getting home.' A grin lighting his face, he said, 'I must say your toast is a tad better than your cheesecake, based solely on presentation. Perhaps I'll make a chef out of you after all. Shop manager, cook, dog walker and carer. The world will be your oyster when you've added all that lot to your CV.' Joe gave a wide yawn.

'Just let me find the car keys,' said Ellie, rummaging through her bag.

'It's okay. I'll walk. I could do with a bit of time to think. And if you're with me, I shall be distracted.' As if drawn together by a magnet, the two embraced, hugging each other tightly.

7

Ellie had been unable to sleep, thinking of Joe walking back on his own, about the fire, and whether or not the restaurant would open as planned. They hadn't even discussed when Ellie would be working at the shop, so she decided to go for half past eight and hoped that would be all right.

As soon as she walked in she realised something wasn't right. Jane was surrounded by paperboys and girls and was hurriedly trying to get their bags packed with the correct newspapers.

'We're gonna be late for school.'

'Can we use this as an excuse?'

'No, just get cracking and you'll only be half an hour late. If any of you would rather get straight to school go now, your wages won't be docked as it was our fault.' She glared at Ellie.

One of the boys slung his bag back

on the counter. 'I'm going to school.' This was followed by cries of 'Me too' and 'I'm off'. The phone rang and Jane picked up immediately.

'I'm very sorry. Your paper is on its way right now.' When she'd finished the call she handed one of the bags to Ellie. 'That's the first one. Nothing like this has ever happened before. Several customers have already rung making complaints. Mr Baines would be furious. Joe said he and you would do the papers this morning. It's my day off. The first I knew about the trouble was when one of the children rang and said they'd been waiting an hour and no one had turned up to open the shop and sort the papers. I'll look after the shop now, but you'd better get going.'

'I don't know any of the streets.'

Jane turned and pulled a map down from a display. 'They're all on there.'

Ellie trudged off, feeling cross and sorry for herself. It wasn't her fault she hadn't known what was supposed to be happening. Joe hadn't told her, but then he'd had other things on his mind. By the time she was on her fourth bag she was feeling even crosser, especially as several people had come out of the houses to complain about the lateness of their papers. As she was trudging back to the shop to collect yet another load, she heard a shout. Joe was running up behind her, a bag slung over his shoulder. 'I'm really sorry, Ellie. I couldn't sleep so when I finally dozed off I completely missed my alarm. When I woke up I went straight to the shop. Jane was in a foul mood until I told her what had happened at the restaurant. She feels awful about having a go at you. She was furious because she was meant to be at Phyllis's this morning to help with breakfast and was upset she'd let her down.'

'I see.' Ellie was still miffed.

'The papers are all done now. I've just finished two rounds, so how about I look after the shop while you and Jane go for a coffee. My treat.'

'I'm not sure I want to go anywhere

with Jane, and shouldn't you be at the restaurant to see what the investigations are showing?' Ellie was more sure than ever that Mick had caused the fire and Jane was somehow in on it, although she knew that was being unfair, as there was no evidence to back it up.

When they walked into the shop Jane looked sheepish. 'I'm very sorry, Ellie. I was out of order. Joe explained what happened last night and how you didn't know what time to turn up. Please forgive me?'

'I suppose so, but my feet are killing me. I wore these sandals because I thought I'd be standing around in the shop, not walking miles and miles.'

'Here, take this.' Joe took a note from the till. 'Go and have a treat at Vanessa's.'

'But like I said, Joe, what about the fire? Don't you want to go and see what's going on?'

'They'll get in touch as soon as they know anything. I'd rather be here keeping busy.' The phone rang.

'That will be another complaint. You'll be answering the phone all morning.' Jane smiled at Joe.

Ellie was pleased to sit in the pretty café and be waited on by Vanessa. She decided to indulge in a chocolate croissant and Jane ordered the same. She also decided to find out whatever she could about Mick. 'Isn't it awful about the fire? Joe was really upset.'

'I'm not surprised. Mick said the restaurant was nearly ready inside and he'd pretty much finished his work there.'

'Does he have other work? I know times are tough for small businesses.'

'Yes. After Joe had asked him to do his electrics he had a call from a big firm. They install security systems in shops and offices. They offered him a contract. We didn't tell Joe, but Mick refused it so that he could do the work he'd promised at the restaurant. He didn't feel he could let Joe down. We've known him all his life. Luckily the security firm couldn't get all the staff they needed so they'll be happy to take Mick on in a week or so. It's good money so a big relief for us.'

Now it didn't seem very likely that Mick could be the culprit, but Ellie would keep an open mind until she'd heard the cause of the fire.

'To make up for my bad temper this morning, I'll teach you the ropes at the shop if you like. When we've finished here we could go back and let Joe have some time to himself. He's a hard worker and hasn't had much free time since his parents went away.'

'I expect he's got a lot of friends to go out with.' Ellie knew she shouldn't fish for information about Joe, but she'd like to know more about his relationship with Amber.

'Loads, but he's never really had a serious relationship. Not as far as I know, anyway. Unless . . . I think that Amber went out with him for a while. I didn't ask him about it, but she gave the impression they were mad about each other whenever she came in the shop and talked to me.'

'What happened?'

'No idea. Do you fancy another croissant or something else? Let's make the most of Joe's treat.'

Ellie suddenly remembered something. 'Joe said you were supposed to be at Phyllis's this morning. Shall I go now?'

'It's fine. I rang her to let her know what happened. She'd already had breakfast. How she managed that, I've no idea.'

★　★　★

Jane's way of initiating Ellie into the role of shop manager was to throw her in at the deep end. When they arrived back, Joe was grateful for a break and Jane immediately suggested Ellie go behind the counter and carry on serving the queue of customers. With Jane beside her, Ellie tried to relax and get on with things.

'You're new here,' said one customer.

'Nice to see another smiling face.'

'We heard the fire engine last night. Rumour has it Joe's restaurant was in trouble. Poor chap, hope things weren't too bad for him,' commiserated another.

Ellie didn't know how to respond to that, so she kept quiet. There was nothing to implicate in the previous night's dramatic events. She took the money, handed over the change and turned to the next shopper.

'Can I help you?'

'Diane,' cried Jane, descending on the woman. 'Haven't seen you for a while. How's Phyllis? Did she tell you I let her down, is that why you're here?'

'Calm down, Jane. Phyllis is fine. She should have told you I arrived last night. I've just come for some supplies, that's all.'

'This is Phyllis's niece,' said Jane by way of introduction. 'And this is Ellie.'

'I was hoping you'd be here in the shop,' said Diane Thompson. 'It was most kind of you to look after Phyllis last week. We had a lovely holiday. It was good to spend time with the grandchildren.'

Ellie was pleased to meet Susan's mother, but she was conscious of the queue of people forming behind her. 'Shall I see to these customers and then we can talk?'

Diane and Jane moved out of the way and Ellie no longer had her adviser nearby. In her usual pragmatic way, she got on with the job until someone wanted to pay by plastic. Then she had to call Jane for a lesson on what to key into the till for the transaction.

At last the shop emptied and the three women were able to chat.

'I'm surprised to see you here,' admitted Ellie to Diane. 'Phyllis said you were going back to work this week.'

'I was, but I thought I'd better make sure things were all right. Phyllis is a good one for saying she's all right when she's not. She had no idea I was coming. I didn't warn her as I knew she'd put me off. Phyllis told me all about your return to Fairsands after I arrived last night.'

'I had a rude awakening when I got back home. Given the sack by a text message. Can you believe that?'

'Actually, yes,' smiled Diane. 'Not everyone's as polite and civil as we would like them to be.'

Ellie explained that Joe had asked her to help out and that was why she had returned. Then she asked after Susan. 'I'll give her a ring and let her know I'm here and that we've met. That'll surprise her.'

'She'd like that. And I understand you and Joe organised a rota of people to call in on Phyllis and Ludo. Very enterprising of you.' Diane smiled and placed her wire basket on the counter.

'I would have been at Phyllis's to get her breakfast if it hadn't been for the fire,' said Jane.

★ ★ ★

The rest of the morning passed quickly and Ellie was surprised and pleased to see Joe enter the shop. She looked up from the till and smiled at him, but he appeared preoccupied as he went over to speak with Jane. Jane! Shouldn't she have gone home by now? thought Ellie. She felt guilty for having Jane around all this time to help her get used to the shop, but then she remembered Phyllis saying they needed extra money, so perhaps the overtime had been a blessing in disguise for her. Then Ellie remembered something else Phyllis had said about Jane not being keen on visiting her.

'You must have a break,' said Joe, coming over to her. 'I'm back to being a shopkeeper now.'

'How are things at the restaurant?' Ellie asked as she came out from behind the counter.

'Not too good, as a matter of fact.' Although Joe attempted a light-hearted tone and tried to smile, Ellie noticed his pale face and the tight line of his mouth. He whispered in her ear, his breath tickling her skin so she shivered. 'I'll tell you later.'

Ellie and Jane left the shop together. 'Thanks for your help, Jane,' said Ellie. 'I wasn't looking forward to my first day, but it's been pleasant so far, apart from the paper round.'

Jane was friendly, but it seemed to Ellie she just wanted to get away.

'Sorry to have delayed you,' added Ellie. 'And if you're finding visiting Phyllis takes too much of your time, I'm happy to be added to the rota of helpers now that I'm back.'

'Oh, would you?' A smile transformed Jane's face. 'I'd be really grateful. It's just that we've — that is, I've got a lot of things going on. I don't want to let Phyllis down, but I'm finding it a bit of a struggle what with everything else . . . ' Her voice trailed off.

'Consider it done. I'm going for a walk along the seafront now. See you tomorrow.' Ellie strode off, puzzled as to what Jane could have meant. Then she shrugged her shoulders and chided herself for being so suspicious; it was perfectly reasonable that Jane should be busy.

The afternoon in the shop was quiet. Joe didn't hang around, but did say he'd call on Ellie that evening and told her to ring his mobile if she came upon any snag in the shop.

A man approached the counter and Ellie smiled a welcome.

'Is Joe around?'

'Not just now. Can I help?' The man looking at her was very attractive in an obvious way: lean, tanned features and a dazzling white smile. 'It's about his parents' caravan. I'll call back.' He turned to leave.

'Just a minute. Do you mean the pretty green and white one at the end of the row on the site over there?' Ellie pointed in the direction of her new home.

The man let out a roar of laughter. 'I haven't heard it described quite as charmingly as that before, but yes. Why?'

'I live there now.' Ellie felt herself responding to the easy manner of the stranger. 'There's nothing wrong, is there?' Fleetingly, Ellie envisaged another fire or worse.

'Not as far as I know. Someone was asking if it was available for a couple of weeks and I said I'd make enquires.' He extended his hand. 'Owen Wilde.'

'Ellie Montgomery.' Their hands met just as Joe returned to the shop.

'What are you doing here?' Joe clenched his fists.

'Enjoying the company of your charming assistant.' With that, Owen winked at Ellie and left the shop.

'What did he want?' Joe asked.

'Someone he knows was asking about the caravan. But what are *you* doing here? I didn't think I'd see you until this evening.' She could tell there was something wrong.

'I hoped I could share the findings of the investigations with you.'

'Of course you can, Joe. What did they say?' Ellie hoped none of her suspicions that it was a premeditated act of sabotage would be confirmed. Perhaps it would turn out to be a simple accident.

'The fire was started deliberately.' Joe's mouth was set in a firm line.

Dismayed, Ellie asked, 'Who'd do such a thing? Was it the electrics?'

'No. It's quite scary really.' Joe took both her hands in his. 'Someone went into the kitchen and set light to one of the bins. All while we were there enjoying the first course.'

'That's awful. Why?'

'I don't know.'

Ellie couldn't believe that Amber would do such a thing. But then again, if she was jealous of Ellie's growing friendship with Joe, maybe she acted on impulse without thinking of the severity of what she was doing. She decided not to mention Amber's name to Joe, at least not until she'd thought about it all a bit more.

Joe gripped her hands harder. 'We need to be careful. It may have been a random act, but if not, someone is out to get one of us. I'm not sure about you being in the caravan on your own.'

'Don't be silly; I'll be fine. Anyway, no one knows I'm living there except a few friends. Oh, yes, and Owen.'

'Owen? I think you should be careful of him too.'

'He seemed charming.'

'Oh he's charming all right. I'll see you tomorrow. You know all about locking up.' Joe left the shop without another word.

Ellie was sorry he'd forgotten his promise to call on her that evening, but she would make the best of things and have a quiet time reading.

When she arrived back at the caravan a large bouquet lay on the top step. She grinned. Obviously Joe was trying to get back in her good books. She found the little envelope amongst the foliage and carefully opened it. 'Fancy a night out sometime? I'll be in touch. Owen x'.

She sat on the step clutching the flowers. Disappointment flowed through her. If she'd received the same message from Joe she'd feel quite different. She decided she needed a chat so threw the flowers back on the step and set off to see Phyllis.

★   ★   ★

'I don't like the sound of that,' Phyllis said after she'd been told how the fire had started.

'It's worrying and in a totally different league from the smashed cake and broken plant pot.'

'Now I'm more convinced that the bike brakes were deliberately damaged and it wasn't just wear and tear. Ellie, dear, I'm rather frightened for you.'

'Me? Why would you be scared for me?' Ellie waited for an answer, but Phyllis said nothing and the penny dropped. '*You* think I'm being targeted too! Joe said the same. I have to admit it does seem a possibility.' Once again her thoughts turned to Amber. 'No, it's ridiculous,' she said.

'Does Joe have any ideas as to who could be behind the fire?'

'I don't really know. I didn't ask him, as he was too upset about the damage to the restaurant, and then he was cross about a man called Owen being in the shop.'

'Owen Wilde? I'm not surprised he was cross. Stay well clear of him.' Phyllis pulled a face.

'I thought he was very nice. And he sent me some flowers. He wants to go out with me.'

'Ellie, really! Tell him to get lost.'

Ellie was surprised at the vehemence in Phyllis's voice and decided to change the subject. 'Where's Ludo?'

'He's a funny old boy. When Diane's here he sticks to her like glue. He's such a loyal dog usually, but I don't mind him making a fuss of her. She's very good to me. They're out for a walk at the moment. When Diane goes to bed he'll be up there lying next to her.'

'That's sweet. Talking of bed, I'd better make a move.'

'I think you should stay here tonight. I don't like the idea of you making your way back to that lonely caravan. We can make up the settee for you.'

'Don't worry about me. I'm going to continue as normal. Whoever is carrying out these attacks isn't going to stop me doing just what I want to do.'

'Well at least phone me when you get back to the caravan. I won't be able to sleep otherwise.'

Ellie didn't feel quite so determined on the walk back. If anyone had been watching her they would have thought her actions anything but normal. She scurried from one hiding place to the next, constantly searching for someone following her. By the time she got back to the caravan her heart was pumping fast and her hands were wet with sweat. After locking the door she leant against it and breathed a sigh of relief. She'd trampled Owen's flowers in her haste to get inside, but she didn't care. They meant nothing to her. Pulling herself together, she phoned Phyllis and bravely told her the walk back had been lovely and she was perfectly fine. Then she leapt fully clothed into bed and buried herself under the duvet, hoping that she'd fall asleep instantly and nothing would wake her during the night.

8

Rain pattering on the roof wakened Ellie. Even though she'd been terrified when she'd fallen into bed, she'd managed to sleep soundly. Her bedside clock told her it was almost seven. Not wanting to get into trouble with Jane again, she showered and dressed, taking the precaution of wearing trainers in case she had to repeat her papergirl duties. With a cup of tea and a biscuit inside her, she felt ready for anything. Perhaps this morning Joe would be in a more receptive mood and they could find time to be together.

'You're early,' greeted Jane as Ellie pushed open the shop door. There was no one else about and the pile of papers on the table was very small compared with yesterday.

'I wasn't sure what time I was due in.

It looks as if I'm too late to help with the papers.'

'No need. It's not your turn today, Ellie.' Joe smiled as he came through from the back area holding a mug of tea. 'Like one?'

Ellie shook her head. 'Where shall I start?'

'Shelf filling,' said Jane. 'There's just been a delivery. Would you mind? It will get you used to where everything is.'

That was fine with Ellie and she started her task. Joe followed her around the aisles. 'I must get things more organised for you,' he said. 'I'm not usually this slapdash. Anyway, Tommy's wife is coming in later this morning and she will serve the customers. She's done it before when I've been shorthanded. With Diane around to walk Ludo, she volunteered to help me out. When she gets here, we'll go somewhere quiet and make plans.'

Tommy's wife, Gwyneth, was as thin and pale as Tommy was red and round.

They both had cheery smiles, though, and Ellie was sure she'd get on well with her. 'I'm so pleased to meet you. You're no stranger to this job, I understand.'

'I worked in a shop before I married Tommy and off and on since. It's nice meeting people. And I'd like to say how sorry I am for the trouble you seem to have been going through since arriving here.' She shook her head from side to side, her blonde curls bouncing. 'Tommy doesn't go into details about his work, but I've learnt to read between the lines.'

'If it's all right with you, we'll head off. Jane, make sure you go on time today. And Gwyneth, if you need me, ring my mobile,' said Joe.

Ellie assumed they were going to the café, but Joe headed off towards the beach. At the rate he was walking and the distance he was covering, she was glad to have her feet clad in trainers. She was also pleased that the skies were brightening and the rain had stopped.

At last Joe stopped and flopped down on a bench inside a bus shelter near the seafront. He pulled Ellie down beside him. 'That's better. I felt stifled back there.'

Ellie wasn't quite sure what he meant, but waited to see if he'd explain. It was good to sit still and watch the seagulls flying overhead with the sound in the background of the shingle shushing as the waves came to the shore and then retreated. It seemed to relax Joe as well. When she risked a look at him, he gave a grin she hadn't seen for a while: a lovely wide one which reached his eyes.

'I hope you'll forgive me, but I lied to you,' he said. 'We're not going to talk business at all for the next couple of hours. We're going to just be Ellie and Joe. Is that all right with you?'

'It's perfect.' Ellie was enchanted to have been kidnapped in this way. Her anxieties about real or pretend threats and supposed enemies melted away as she let Joe hold her hand in his. They sat together for a while in silence.

'First of all,' said Joe at last, 'I want to explain why I didn't come to see you off when you left Phyllis's to go back home at the weekend. I had a phone call asking me to go to the restaurant as one of the workmen had found a hitch with the flooring.' Joe looked at Ellie. 'By the time I got to Phyllis's I saw you driving off.'

'I was a bit disappointed you didn't turn up.'

'Also, I'm afraid I was in a vile mood yesterday after seeing Wilde. How I could forget I said we'd meet, I've no idea. The next thing I want to say is that I'm sorry our evening at the restaurant was cut short. I hope we can put that right very soon, although it will have to be at some other venue.'

'You could come to the caravan. I've got a good cookbook called *Gourmet Meals from the Microwave*,' joked Ellie.

'I might take you up on that.' Joe raised her hand and brushed it gently with his lips. 'There are a lot of other things reeling round in my head, but I want to forget all about them for the time being.'

After a while, Joe stood up and pulled Ellie beside him. 'Shall we walk?'

As they did so, Joe talked about the amenities in Fairsands and gave Ellie a feel of the town which was to become her home for the next few weeks. 'Everyone seems to know you,' she said. 'Were you born here?'

'Yes. When I left school I travelled a bit, but still couldn't bring myself to permanently leave. The cookery course wasn't far away. Then when Mum and Dad talked about a retirement plan of going on a cruise, I thought it would be nice for them to go now. Why wait?'

'So you stepped into the breach with the shop.' Ellie felt more than admiration for Joe. He was unselfish, a quality she wished there was more of. 'Don't you mind the long hours?'

Joe shrugged. 'Not much I could do about it even if I did. It should stand me in good stead with the restaurant anyway. I'll have staff working with me, of course, but I want to be a hands-on owner.'

'It's a shame things have to be put back,' said Ellie. 'I understand Amber will be working for you.'

Joe looked bemused. 'Amber? No, why do you say that?'

Not wanting to go into detail, but feeling relieved, Ellie just said, 'I must have got hold of the wrong end of the stick. Sorry, you didn't want to talk business.'

'Not now anyway. Although there is something I need help with. I'm trying to come up with a name for the restaurant. Any ideas? I quite like Acute Angle.'

'Will people get it? How about Lazy Faire?'

'That's good. Let's stop for a moment and take in the view.'

Ellie stared out at the sea. 'Blue Horizon! That could be the name for your restaurant.'

'Brilliant idea. At last I can get the signs made. Has all that thinking made you hungry?'

'A bit. Are we going back then?' Ellie felt disappointment, as she was enjoying her time with Joe.

He shook his head. 'Over here.' They were nearly on the beach when Ellie spotted what looked like a row of beach huts. 'Smell that,' said Joe, taking a deep breath.

Ellie laughed delightedly as she saw a white hut just pulling up its shutters. Above the kiosk were the words, 'Fish & Chips'. 'I will not be able to resist a large helping of that. My favourite meal.'

Joe cocked an eye at her. 'Better than anything I've given you?'

'Don't fish for compliments, Joe Baines,' teased Ellie.

The happy couple took their steaming parcels and sat on the sea wall to eat.

'What do you do in your spare time, Ellie?' Joe had finished his food and was licking his lips.

'Oh I'm kept quite busy,' Ellie assured him. 'I get phone calls out of the blue head-hunting me to be a corner shop manager-cum-papergirl, and then I'm whisked off to sea to enjoy gourmet meals. Add a bit of jogging and that's just about me. What about you, Joe? What do you enjoy doing?'

'Spending time with you.' This time there was no accompanying grin on his face as he looked deep into her eyes. This had to be the best day of her life so far, decided Ellie. Then she heard the sweet-sounding voice of Joe singing a love song to her. He lapsed into silence, not finishing off the verse where the singer declares his love.

Hand in hand, they retraced their steps towards the corner shop.

'You know,' said Joe, 'we still haven't sorted out your hours and other things to do with the shop. Not very business-like of me, is it? If you're happy to be flexible, shall we see how things go?'

'Suits me. I've nothing else planned.

I'll come in each morning about the time I did today unless I'm told anything different.'

When they reached the shop, Ellie was surprised to see Phyllis sitting on a chair near the counter chatting away to Gwyneth.

'I was waiting for you, Joe,' said Phyllis, starting to rise from the chair. 'I hear you're in a bit of a predicament with manning the shop. I've come to volunteer.'

'How kind,' said Joe. 'Have you experience of this kind of work?'

Phyllis's face fell. 'Not directly, but I'm sure I'd be able to pick it up. I've seen what goes on from the customer's point of view.'

'I see. Well, would you like to see how you get on?'

'What, now?' Phyllis looked eager.

Ellie wasn't sure what was going on. How on earth could Joe even consider Phyllis as an employee, considering not only her age, but her injury?

'Come round behind the counter. I

expect Gwyneth could do with a break.'

Joe scurried around the shop, popping a few random items into a basket and presenting it at the till. 'See how you manage with these.' He smiled encouragingly at Phyllis.

To give her her due, thought Ellie, she was doing well. She watched as the older woman scanned the tub of margarine and the bread. Then she tried to lift the bag of potatoes, but they dropped with a thud. Resolutely, she pushed them to one side, picked up the multipack of tinned beans, and struggled with them. She sighed. 'I'm not doing well, am I?'

'On the contrary, you're doing extremely well,' smiled Joe. 'I think you're a bit hampered by the plaster on your arm. Perhaps when that's removed, you'll come back and have another go. What do you say?'

Ellie could have hugged Joe. With tact, he'd maintained Phyllis's dignity. She loved him more than ever. A dizzy feeling came over her. *Did* she love Joe Baines? There was no time to answer her own question, as Phyllis was addressing her.

'Diane's just taken me to the optician. He agrees with what you said about my bifocal glasses and I'm having two new pairs made up. He also said that if you want a job, you can work for him.'

'I think Ellie will have enough to do working here,' laughed Joe. 'I must disappear now.' He turned to Ellie. 'I'll be back at about five or six if you can hold the fort until then. You've got my mobile number. Don't hesitate to ring if there's a problem.'

Ellie was quite content to be looking after the shop on her own that afternoon. A few customers came and went and she was pleased to be getting to know the locals. Her time spent stacking the shelves also proved handy when somebody wanted to know the whereabouts of stock. It made a nice change from an office. Although she missed the company of the other workers, Susan in particular, she was not short of acquaintances now. As she tidied the shelf below the counter, she was aware of someone in the shop. Quickly she stood up and got ready to call a greeting. Her heart sank. It was Amber. Despite anything she felt inside her, Ellie was determined to be welcoming; she was a customer after all and she owed it to Joe to be polite.

'Hello, Amber. How are you?'

'I'm looking for Joe. He should be here.' Amber's eyes flitted around the shop and she started to walk towards the private room at the back.

Hastily Ellie barred her way. 'Sorry, he had to go out. Can I help?'

'I don't think so.' Amber almost spat the words, but she stopped in her tracks.

'If it's urgent, you could try ringing him,' suggested Ellie.

'His phone's off.' She let out a sigh. 'It doesn't matter. He'll get in touch later, I'm sure.' And with that, she marched out of the shop, her face like thunder.

Trying to put the incident out of her mind, Ellie returned to her duties. When someone phoned with an order, she scrabbled around for a pen and piece of paper and made a list, making sure she took the name and address of the caller. Then she was informed that the order should be delivered that evening between six and seven. Mentally Ellie worked out that if she packed up the items, Joe could deliver them when he called in as promised.

The clock nudged towards six and there was no sign of Joe. Ellie didn't mind staying at work, but she was worried about the order she'd taken. She didn't want to let anyone down. Perhaps she should ring Joe and find out what to do. He answered on the second ring and Ellie was pleased and relieved to hear his voice. When she explained the situation, he promised to be back as soon as he could.

'Oh, and Amber was here wanting to

speak to you. I suggested she ring you as it sounded urgent, but she said your phone was switched off.' Ellie's conscience felt lighter having got that off her chest.

'Amber hasn't got my number. I changed it after she kept ringing me at any trivial excuse. I'm sure it's not urgent, but thanks for passing on the message. See you soon.'

* * *

Joe didn't stop long when he eventually returned to the shop. He set off with the order Ellie had packed and told her to close the shop at seven.

Back at the caravan, she spied the bouquet of flowers which had got pushed under the steps of the caravan. It was a reminder of Owen, and Phyllis's words of warning. However, the flowers looked so woeful she couldn't help taking pity on them, so she rescued them and popped them in a jug. They brightened the caravan and she tried to forget their association. Still full from the impromptu lunch, Ellie made a cup of tea and decided to take a walk around the immediate vicinity.

'Well, this is nice,' came a voice which put a tingle of fear in Ellie.

'Hello, Owen.' She would be polite, but nothing more. 'Thank you for the flowers.'

'I wondered if you'd accept them. I think I've a bit of a reputation for being a monster.'

'And are you?' Ellie relaxed and tried to keep a smile from her lips, but Owen looked apologetic as he stood in front of her.

'You could take a chance and find out for yourself,' he invited.

'That's not a good idea,' replied Ellie, immediately regretting letting her guard drop. 'I'm going back now. Goodbye.' As she turned and headed towards the sanctuary of her caravan, she tried not to break into a run. It was difficult not to keep looking over her shoulder. If only she hadn't been so stupid as to fall into conversation with him.

Safely back indoors, she locked and bolted the door and was thankful that the windows were far too small to allow anyone to climb through, even someone of Owen's build.

When a knock came at the door, Ellie shivered and immersed herself in her book, trying to pretend nothing untoward was happening. Her hand gripped her phone, but who could she call? Joe was exhausted and had worries of his own. At last the knocking stopped. Owen must have got the message. Despite what Phyllis implied, it wasn't likely that anyone was really out to hurt Ellie.

She made a drink of hot chocolate and got ready for bed. As she passed the door, her bare foot encountered something. Looking down, she saw a folded piece of paper. So, Owen hadn't entirely given up on her. She picked it up and read the words: I think you are at home, but you must be busy. I need to talk to you. J.

Ellie could have kicked herself. All that wasted effort of worrying and wanting to get in touch with Joe, and he'd been on the other side of the door. The door she had refused to answer.

9

As Ellie stacked tins of beans on a shelf she thought about how quickly she'd become the manager of the shop and with very little help and training. She'd simply been thrown in at the deep end and barely seen Joe. When he had come into the shop her heart had flipped a little, then she'd got herself under control, behaved in a business-like way, and talked about stock control and orders. The time they'd eaten fish and chips sitting on the wall together seemed to have happened in another life and definitely more than two weeks ago. Sometimes when Joe rushed in to sort something he'd stop and give her one of his melting smiles and tell her they must do something together, but the restaurant kept him busy.

'They look right. You don't need to fiddle with them anymore.'

'Phyllis! How are you today?'

'Very well, thank you, but I'll have a sit-down if you don't mind. I haven't seen you for a few days. I wondered if you'd like to come to the opening night of the restaurant with me and a few of the others. I'll book a table. Unless Joe's already asked you.'

'I've hardly seen him.'

'I suppose he'll be too busy working to be able to sit down and have a meal with you. Maybe he'll ask you another evening when things have calmed down a bit. They've all been working very hard to get it finished. Mick's been there all hours. How's Jane?'

'I think me coming here has upset her. She cut down her hours almost as soon as I started.'

'How very odd.' Phyllis frowned.

'Why do you say that?'

'I shouldn't gossip, but I think I can trust you not to tell anyone. They moved to a bigger house a short while ago and took on a large mortgage. Unfortunately, they've been struggling.

159

I would have thought Jane would want all the hours she could get in the shop. She doesn't come and see me anymore either. How very worrying. They're a lovely family. I wouldn't want to think they're in further difficulties. Oh, look who's here!'

Joe grinned at the two women as he came through the door. ''Morning, ladies. I hope you're both excited at the prospect of the latest opening in Fairsands. You'll both be my guests on the evening.'

'No, we certainly won't. We'll come as proper diners, pay our way and then we can say just what we want about the ambience and food.' Phyllis patted him on the arm.

'It's no good trying to bribe you two then. I'll have to try elsewhere.' Joe chuckled as he wandered into the back office. He returned shortly afterwards. 'Everything looks perfect. I had a quick glance at the important documents on the computer and my new manager appears to know what she's doing.'

Ellie felt a warm glow at his praise. 'We were talking about Jane. We think it's a bit odd that she's cut her hours and isn't visiting Phyllis. How's Mick?'

'He's a hard worker, but I don't spend time with him socially. I did hear from someone else that he'd been offered a big contract with a security firm and had declined it to do the work for me. That was very good of him and I'm pleased they are still willing to take him on when he's finished my work.'

'Jane told me that too. Maybe that's why she can afford to cut her hours.' Ellie straightened some packets of biscuits.

'Whatever is she doing with her time?' Phyllis frowned. 'She's one of these people who can't sit still and likes to be kept busy. And it's not like her to ignore her friends. None of our business though.'

Ellie almost giggled. It seemed to her that everybody's business *was* discussed in the shop, but she tried hard not to listen or become involved.

Joe was at the door. 'So I'll see you two at the opening.'

'Oh, he's gone. I'm sure you'll see him before then, dear. Now, how about helping me with my shopping. To start with I need some dried fruit.'

★　★　★

Ellie looked in the mirror and was pleased she'd made an effort with her outfit and hair. She'd found a pretty print dress in the charity shop and teamed it with a fitted jacket and flat shoes. Her hair had behaved itself and was smooth and sleek with no sticking-out bits. A perfect bob. She'd decided to make her own way to the Blue Horizon and meet Phyllis, Tommy and the others there for the champagne reception. Not that she needed champagne — excitement bubbled through her already.

As she opened the door she looked up at the beautiful evening sky with white clouds backlit by the sun to silver.

The next thing she knew she was tumbling to the ground. She groaned and pulled herself up to a sitting position. Her ankle hurt. She rubbed at it to ease the pain. Telling herself she'd be all right, she took some deep breaths and tried to relax. How stupid she was to step into nothing. But what had happened to the steps? They were lying nearby and looked as if they'd been knocked over.

After hauling herself up to standing, she righted the steps and put them in the correct position. Then she hobbled back inside. She slumped on the bench seat and leant on the table. It was then that she realised her face was bleeding slightly and that she must have grazed it when she fell. She decided to make a cup of tea and then see if she could sort herself out enough to get to the restaurant in time for the meal at least. If she couldn't hobble then she'd call a taxi.

As she drained her cup there was a knock at the door. 'Hello, are you here?'

'Come in.' Ellie was relieved to hear the familiar voice.

Joe's face showed concern. 'What's happened, Ellie? You've had an accident.'

'I fell from the caravan. The steps had been knocked over and I wasn't looking down.' She gestured towards her ankle, which was puffing up quite dramatically. Then she put her hand to her face trying to conceal the messy blood trickling towards her chin.

'Oh, Ellie.' He rushed over and took her in his arms. 'This is awful. I wish I hadn't asked you to come back to Fairsands. Everything goes wrong for you here.' He stroked her hair and studied her face, gently pulling her hand away. 'I'll get something to clean your cheek with.'

'Don't worry, I'll see to it. You get back. You can't spend time here looking after me on your important big night.'

'You're more important than my restaurant. Do you feel up to joining the others? They're all very concerned about you. Phyllis said it's not like you not to turn up. She knew something had happened.'

'She's a dear.'

'Not your first impression.' They both smiled. 'You get yourself ready and we'll walk back together.'

'I'm not sure I can. I sprained my ankle.'

'Mmm, I have an idea. I just need a few bits and pieces. I'll be back in two minutes.' He rushed away, his arms full of colourful cushions and blankets.

Ellie sponged her face and changed into some trousers and a sparkly top. Her new dress had a rip in the skirt and the jacket had a dirty mark down one sleeve. Just as she'd made the decision to go barefoot, Joe was back. 'Your carriage, m'lady,' he said, pointing at a wheelbarrow draped with the blankets and bedecked with cushions.

'You *are* joking.'

'Take my arm and I'll help you in.'

Joe sang as he pushed Ellie along the seafront. Ellie would never have thought this scenario could be romantic, but with the looks Joe was giving her and the words he was singing she couldn't have thought of a more romantic form of transport. He pushed her all the way up the wheelchair ramp and into the restaurant, where she was greeted with cheers and smiles. Joe helped her out of the wheelbarrow and left her with their friends while he went to see how the kitchen staff were getting on.

'You have been in the wars, dear,' Phyllis said, scrutinising her face. 'Come and sit next to me and tell me all about it.' After she'd told the story, Phyllis took her hand. 'I imagine those steps are metal and too heavy to blow anywhere.'

'They are. You're thinking along the same lines as me. The steps were knocked over deliberately, weren't they?'

'I believe they were. Now who wouldn't have wanted you here this evening?' Phyllis asked. As one they both looked around for Amber, and there she was clutching Joe's arm and talking to him animatedly. Phyllis scowled. 'I don't think we need Tommy's expert help, but you will have to talk to Joe and tell him what we think.'

Ellie was already wishing she'd pretended her injuries were worse so that she could have stayed at home. That would have spared her the pain of seeing Joe with another woman. Amber reached up and kissed him on the lips. Joe took her hand and led her to a table, fussing round her with drinks. Ellie couldn't bear to watch. One minute he'd been singing romantically to her and the next he was all over another woman. Was he the sort of man she wanted? All she knew was that she'd fallen head over heels in love with him, and if he didn't care for her, she didn't know what she would do.

There was plenty of lively chat to keep Ellie's mind occupied and she was intrigued when Chris brought up the subject of yet more development in the town.

'I heard a rumour in the office that

the developer bloke wants to buy the caravan site.'

'What use would that be to him? He won't be allowed to build houses or anything else there, will he, Chris?' Phyllis looked across the table at Vanessa's husband.

'As far as I know, nothing major. But there is the possibility of developing the site — putting in more facilities like a clubhouse, small funfair, a children's playground and other amenities.'

'But it's so lovely and peaceful there,' Ellie exclaimed. 'You can hear nothing but nature.'

Chris sighed. 'He doesn't care about that sort of thing. All he cares about is making money. As soon as he knew the decision about the amusement arcade he started looking for another project. It's possible the owner won't sell.'

'I'll have a word with her tomorrow. My family have known hers all our lives. I'm sure she won't be willing to sell once she knows what's going on. But let's forget all that now and enjoy Joe's food. This chocolate raspberry tart looks delicious.' Phyllis tucked in.

Ellie was aware of Joe visiting each table and he was soon standing behind her chair. After a brief conversation with the others he bent down and whispered in her ear. 'I'll run you home when you're ready. Better go before your wheelbarrow turns into a pumpkin. I'll be back shortly.'

The idea of a return trip with Joe singing as he pushed her along appealed, but then she remembered how he and Amber had looked so close earlier. When Tommy offered to push her home she accepted and was whisked off before Joe reappeared. It was for the best, she told herself.

* * *

By the morning, Ellie's ankle was less swollen and a bruise coloured her leg. She had to get to work; she didn't want to let Joe down in spite of his behaviour the previous evening. It was obvious she couldn't drive and there was no way she was waiting to see if anyone would turn up with a wheelbarrow. At that thought, she giggled to herself. No one had seemed to think it remotely odd that she'd arrived for dinner at the Blue Horizon in that mode of transport. Despite strange happenings at Fairsands, she was growing more fond of it each day.

After she had showered and dressed, she phoned for a taxi to take her to the shop. When she stepped out of the caravan, she made sure the steps were in place. A grey cloud passed across her as she remembered her accident of the evening before.

The taxi driver was very kind and helped her into the car, commenting that his wife was a regular customer at the shop. Ellie perked up a bit as she chatted to him; she was sure she could manage the day ahead, especially if Jane or Gwyneth were around to help.

'I'm pleased you're here and I'm glad

to see you sitting down. What did you think of the evening?' Joe asked on entering the shop later that morning.

'It was fantastic and the food was delicious, but you don't need me to tell you that. It's what everyone is saying.'

'Do I look smug?'

'Very.' Ellie liked their easy banter, but at the back of her mind there was Amber.

'I'm sorry I missed taking you home. You disappeared so quickly.'

'I was well looked after. Now I need to see to the bread order if you'll excuse me.' Ellie hobbled into the back and started working at the computer.

Joe followed. 'I feel as though I've done something wrong. I thought we were getting on so well, but you've cooled off since the meal last night.'

Ellie stopped working and looked up at him. 'I like you, Joe, and I thought we were getting on well too, but I saw you with Amber last night and it seems clear there's more going on there than you admitted to.'

'I don't know what you're talking about.'

'Amber kissed you. You fussed around her as though she meant a lot to you. But you told me you'd finished with her and there was nothing going on. I'd prefer you to be honest with me.'

'I *am* being honest. She's so persistent. I told you the truth. I went out with her, but it was a mistake. I fussed around her as you call it because I wanted to get her sitting down so that I could escape. She kissed me. Did you see me kissing her? No, you didn't, because I don't want to. Ever. The person I want to kiss is right here. Ellie, it's you I want to . . . ' As Joe leaned down towards her, the shop doorbell jangled and Ellie leapt up with a wince to deal with the customer.

The moment was lost, but Ellie believed what he'd said was the truth and a great wave of happiness flooded through her. Joe held the door open for the customer. 'I'd better be going,' said Joe.

'How about that meal I promised you at the caravan? I can't guarantee it will be up to Blue Horizon standards, but I'll do my best.' Ellie hoped Joe would agree to let her cook for him. She also hoped there would be an opportunity to pick up where he left off when he acknowledged he wanted to kiss her.

'I'd love to come. For the time being we're not opening the restaurant on Mondays so would next Monday suit you?'

'Lovely. That will give me time to go round and ask Phyllis for some advice. She's got loads of cook books and heaps of tips. I think I need all the help I can get in the kitchen.' Ellie hoped she hadn't put Joe off by saying that, but he didn't appear daunted.

'That's one of the things I love about you. You don't pretend to be anything you're not.'

For the rest of the day Joe's words jumped around her mind — 'that's one of the things I love about you.'

★ ★ ★

Ellie sang as she laid the table. She'd been a bit embarrassed to arrive at Phyllis's house in a taxi. It had been impossible for her to take Ludo for a walk, but Phyllis had waved aside her apologies and insisted on making Ellie comfortable on the settee. They'd had a gossip about Joe's opening of Blue Horizon and agreed he would make a success of it if his hard work and attention to detail were anything to go by. He had been a wonderful host and his food was superb. Ellie told her of the plan to make Joe a nice meal at the caravan and asked her advice about what to cook which even she couldn't mess up. Phyllis had been eager to impart information and guidance, insisting it was good to feel useful after being waited on by people for so long.

Ellie had picked a few flowers at Phyllis's which were now displayed in a little glass bottle in the centre of the table. The meal they'd chosen was simple and plain, but Phyllis had still read through the recipes with her and explained each step. Ellie felt confident that she'd produced a meal to be proud of.

The knock at the door made her start. It wasn't eight yet and she hadn't expected Joe to arrive early.

'Come in,' she called. 'Oh, Owen, I wasn't expecting you.'

'This looks nice and cosy.' Owen scanned the table.

'I'm expecting Joe any minute.' Ellie hoped Owen would be gone before Joe arrived. She didn't want the evening to start badly.

'Baines is coming, is he? Has he dumped his other girlfriend?'

Ellie felt uncomfortable. She didn't want to discuss Joe's private matters with an almost stranger. She decided not to speak.

'What about that date you promised me?' he asked.

'I don't think I promised you anything. You can see I'm busy right now.

Another time perhaps.' She opened the door wide.

'I'll hold you to that.'

She watched him go. He was very attractive in an eye-catching way, but there was something about him which made her wary. Happy that Joe hadn't seen Owen at the caravan, she put the finishing touches to the meal. When Joe arrived a few minutes later he looked like thunder.

'I met Owen Wilde. He said he'd been here and you're going to go out with him.'

'That's ridiculous, Joe. I didn't invite him here and I didn't want him here.'

'But you like him.'

'I don't know him. Please don't spoil our evening. Phyllis and I have been working hard.'

Joe's anger abated. 'Sorry. I'll go out and arrive again.' Ellie watched in amusement as Joe exited the caravan and shut the door behind him. Then she heard a knock and the second time he came in he kissed her on both cheeks. 'Lovely to see you.'

'You too. If you'll take a seat I'll serve the first course. It's smoked mackerel pâté on sour rye bread with a watercress garnish. Shall we have white wine with it?'

'Perfect.'

You are as well, thought Ellie. *In my eyes, anyway.* Sure she was blushing, Ellie ducked her head and tasted the pâté.

'Mmm, that was good,' Joe said, before leaning back contentedly.

'If you'll just give me a moment I'll serve the main course.' Ellie cleared the plates and removed a baking tin from the oven.

'That looks impressive. And it smells wonderful.'

'I think you can probably smell the thyme. I've made shallot tarte tatin with goat's cheese. I'm serving it with a green salad. I hope that's all right.'

'Fantastic. Did Phyllis really help you with the menu?'

'Yes, I wouldn't have tried this

without her encouragement. She's been looking through a lot of magazines since her accident and tore out some recipes, including this one. But I have to confess I didn't make the puff pastry.'

'Life's too short to make puff pastry,' smiled Joe. 'So long as you got it from Baines's, that's fine by me.'

★   ★   ★

'That was all delicious.' Joe sipped his coffee. 'You and Phyllis make a good team.'

'I'll tell her.'

'That summer pudding was one of the best I've ever tasted.'

Ellie basked in his praise. She was happy with the food she'd prepared.

'I've been thinking. How did you manage to fall out of the caravan? If there's some sort of problem, we need to put it right before you have another accident.'

'Someone wanted me to fall. The

steps had been kicked over. There's no way they were blown away. It wasn't especially windy that day anyway. I wasn't looking and just stepped into thin air.'

'Deliberate!' Joe stood up and went outside. On his return he said, 'You're right. Those steps are far too heavy to be moved by the wind. Who would want to do this?'

Ellie didn't know whether to reply or not. 'Who do you think?'

'I don't know. I'm sorry, but it definitely seems to be you they're targeting.'

'Who would target me? I've only been here a short time and what have I done?'

'You've done nothing except work hard and make me happy.'

Ellie hoped Joe would come to the same conclusion as her if she stayed silent and let him think for a while. And he did. 'Amber. You were right all along. She's jealous of us. There's no one else it could possibly be.'

'I agree. Don't forget your restaurant was set on fire too. Why would she do that?'

'She wouldn't. The investigators think it was a gang of youths from another town. There have been a few similar incidents in nearby towns. They probably took the opportunity to have some fun when they found the kitchen door open and no one in there. That definitely wasn't Amber. I'm convinced of it. But I will speak to her. I'll tell her I'll go to the police about the things she's done to you.' He paced the short space of the caravan.

'No, please, leave it. We have no proof and she hasn't done much harm.'

'Not yet, but we don't know what she might do next. I don't think you should stay here on your own. Why don't you move back in with Phyllis?'

'She wants to be independent. I'm not scared of staying here alone. I know I was before, but I'm not any longer. One day I might catch Amber and once we've got proof we can confront her with it. That should stop her.'

Joe took Ellie in his arms. 'You're brave and sensible. And a fantastic cook. I am very pleased you came to Fairsands.' With that he put his hands on her cheeks and looked into her eyes. Ellie could feel waves of love radiating from him and put her lips on his. Nothing could part them now.

10

The following day doubts about Joe crept back. He hadn't mentioned the note he'd popped through the door that evening Ellie had pretended not to be in. Perhaps he wasn't being entirely honest with her, although she hated to have such thoughts. In her bleak moments she imagined Joe had left the note because he wanted to tell her he was seeing Amber again. What was he playing at?

It was her afternoon off and she was planning on catching up with chores in the caravan and reading the romance she'd downloaded to her Kindle.

'Sorry I'm late,' Jane said when she arrived to take over at the shop. 'I'm starving and thirsty. Is there any hot water in the kettle?'

'You sit here and I'll hobble off and

make you a drink.'

'I've got some sandwiches. I just didn't have time to eat them.'

Ellie wondered why Jane had made sandwiches to bring with her when she would probably have come straight from home. Maybe Phyllis was right and something funny *was* going on.

Ellie made two mugs of tea and after putting them on the counter went back to fetch the chair from the office so they could both sit down.

'Thanks, Ellie, you're very kind. Actually, that's why I left that note.'

'Note?'

'At your caravan. I think you were in, just not answering.'

'*You* left the note? I thought it was Joe.'

'I expect you're disappointed.'

'Not at all. I'm relieved.' Ellie sipped her tea.

'I wanted to talk to someone who isn't involved in the town and with everyone else's business. I feel I can trust you to keep quiet. The thing is, the others will think I've acted traitorously. I feel it myself, but I have to do this. Of course Mick knows, but the others will find out soon enough.'

'I've no idea what you're talking about. If you want to tell me, I promise I won't say a word to anyone. I'm sure it can't be as bad as you're making out.'

'I'll start at the beginning. Mick and I moved fairly recently to a bigger house, but his business has been struggling and I didn't earn much here. I was offered a new job with better money so grabbed at it. At the moment I'm only working part-time, but soon I'll finish here completely and work full-time for my new boss. With that and Mick's contract with the security firm, we'll be able to manage the monthly mortgage repayments.'

'I'm sorry, but I don't see the problem. It seems to be perfect.'

'Not at all. You'll have heard about a developer who's trying to make a lot of money from developing Fairsands? I work for him.'

Ellie could see the difficulty now. 'So all your friends will be unhappy.'

'That's why I stopped going to see Phyllis. I felt uncomfortable, and even Ludo sensed my unease. I'm so miserable doing this behind their backs, but when the truth comes out it will be even worse.'

'I can understand your dilemma. Do you enjoy the job?'

'It's what I'm trained for. Accounts. But I will miss the people here in the shop and I don't like some of the dodgy practices which I'm party to. I can hardly report him to the Inland Revenue though, can I?'

'Are there no other jobs?' Ellie knew as soon as she'd said it what a daft question it was. She'd been temping for a while simply because there had been so little permanent work. 'I'm really sorry you're miserable. I've no idea what to suggest, but I do think your friends would understand if you explained as you have to me.'

'I'll keep looking for another job that

pays as well, but for the time being I'll have to stay there. I'll keep out of everyone's way. I may go shopping in the supermarket because I always bump into someone here. I think that might work — avoiding everyone.'

★　★　★

Ellie was bothered by Jane's revelation. She would stick to her promise not to tell anyone, but wished she could share the burden with Joe. He'd come up with some plan she was sure. When her phone rang she was surprised and pleased to hear Joe's voice. 'I'm checking up on your foot,' he said.

'Well, it's far less painful and hardly swollen at all, although I don't think I could run a marathon.'

'But you might be up to taking a little gentle exercise along the beach?'

'That would be lovely,' sighed Ellie. 'I could do with some air and it's beautiful outside.'

'I'll be with you in a short while. By

the way, I've got company.'

That bit wasn't quite so good, thought Ellie, desperately hoping it wasn't Amber. Surely Joe wouldn't do that. She washed her face in cool water and pulled a brush through her hair. She was a bit fed up with wearing trainers, but they were the most comfortable footwear she had and a walk along the beach didn't warrant anything more fashionable.

When she opened the door, she bent down to let herself be licked by Ludo, who was struggling to get up the steps and nearer to her. 'Good boy. Are we taking you for a walk?'

'Phyllis said you'd like to join us,' said Joe.

'Oh, I'm an afterthought, am I?' Ellie couldn't believe she was being so uncharitable to Joe.

'Not at all,' he replied, not looking put out at all. 'I wasn't sure how you'd feel about exercise, that's all.' He put his arm around her shoulder and kissed her cheek. 'We needn't go far.'

The three of them sauntered off at a leisurely pace, Joe showing Ellie yet another hidden path to the beach around the back of the caravan site. He tucked her arm through his and when the sea was in sight, he began singing. Ellie loved listening to his rich voice, not caring what song he sang. After a while he stopped singing and hummed quietly.

'Is everything all right, Joe?' She had the feeling he was preoccupied.

'What makes you ask?' He stopped and pulled her towards him. 'As a matter of fact, I've been thinking about the restaurant and the shop and you.'

'All at the same time?' teased Ellie. She was pleased he was opening up to her, but he sounded serious.

'I don't seem to have much time to spend with you. I couldn't bear to lose you.'

'We'll be all right, Joe,' Ellie assured him. 'We can get to know each other slowly. But for now, shall we enjoy our walk?'

'Thanks,' he said. 'That's just what I hoped you'd say.'

Ludo circled them both and gave a little bark. 'He agrees,' said Ellie with a smile.

When they reached the dunes, Joe flopped down. 'Shall we rest here for a while? I don't want to have to carry you home.'

Ellie was pleased to have a rest, especially at Joe's side. Together they lay in the dunes looking up at the sky, which was dotted with a few fluffy cotton-wool clouds. Beside them, Ludo started digging in the sand, but soon gave up and settled down for a short nap. Ellie hoped that the relaxing atmosphere would let Joe unwind.

When they returned to the caravan, Ellie invited Joe in for a drink.

'No, I'll get Ludo home. Thanks for a lovely walk, Ellie. I'll see you tomorrow.' They shared a hug and Ellie waved him and Ludo off.

★   ★   ★

The next time Phyllis turned up at the shop she was fuming. 'I've been to see Martha and she's thinking of selling the caravan site to that awful man. She says it's too good an offer to turn down, but she's torn because she doesn't want to upset us. Whatever will we do? Joe's parents will be very sad if they come back and find the whole place has been sold and is going to be turned into some sort of holiday park.'

'It might not be too bad.' As soon as she'd spoken the words Ellie knew she'd said the wrong thing.

Phyllis said with an acid edge to her voice, 'There are plenty of places like that along the coast if people want them. Fairsands is different. It's for people who appreciate scenery, the quietness and slow pace of the town, nice places to eat, making their own entertainment. We don't sell 'kiss me quick' hats here.'

'I do know what you mean. I thought maybe this chap who's buying up the site might not make the changes you all fear.'

'Humph.'

'Have a seat, Phyllis. If you give me your list I'll gather up your shopping.' Ellie chatted to Phyllis about other news she'd heard from customers. She hoped to cheer her up, but the older woman was single-minded.

'We're not having it. I'll arrange a meeting and get a petition started. We'll need to deliver leaflets to every house in the town and put posters up wherever we can think of.'

'Are you sure you'll manage all this when you're still recovering from your fall?'

'I'm perfectly well. I've broken my arm, not lost my marbles.'

'Formidable' was the word which sprang into Ellie's mind. The developer would have to be a brave man to take on Phyllis and her friends again. She almost giggled, then thought better of it. 'I'll help in any way I can. I'll happily deliver leaflets. It would be good exercise.'

'Thank you. I'll let you know when they're printed. You can come to the meeting too, so that you know exactly what's going on.'

'Right.' Ellie saw that Phyllis was in her element when she had something to fight for. 'There you are. That's all your shopping.'

'Thank you, dear. Pop it in my trolley for me, will you? Now, tell me how you're getting on with Joe.'

'I told you he enjoyed the meal at the caravan. I haven't seen much of him since then. I'm afraid he's been very busy with the restaurant. He did say that once it was fully staffed he'd have more time. I think it was your idea he collect me when he took Ludo for a walk the other day. We get on well. I feel happy when I'm with him.'

'You want to hang onto him, dear. Don't let that Amber anywhere near him. I don't like her. She sometimes calls to see if I want anything, but I don't spend long with her.'

* ★ *

As she approached the caravan after work, Ellie immediately noticed that the door was banging on its hinges in the breeze. Since living there she'd been careful to close the windows and lock the door each time she went out. She took a deep breath and stepped inside. The interior was a complete mess. Her clothes had been strewn across the bed and her personal possessions had been moved around. She checked her few valuables were still safely hidden away and sighed with relief. It didn't look as if anything had been taken; it was just a wanton act of invasion of her privacy. Her practical side told her to stay and clear up, but she felt like running away. She walked through the site and onto the beach. She was reluctant to leave the caravan openly defenceless, but it was a case of locking the stable door after the horse had bolted. Deciding to chance it, she jogged down to the sea. She began to feel better and her head cleared. The decision had to be made as to whether or not she stayed in Fairsands.

Puffing back towards her home, she found Joe sitting on the steps, a troubled frown creasing his face. 'Where have you been? What's going on? I've been worried sick. Are you all right?' He took her in his arms and hugged her tightly. 'If this is Amber's work,' he jerked his head towards the caravan, 'I'm going to speak to her. She can't keep on doing these things.'

'We still have no proof it's her. I've been thinking. It seems to me she's trying to drive me away, so I've decided to . . .'

'Oh, no, Ellie, you mustn't leave. You must stay and show her that whatever she does it will make no difference to us. If you go she's won.'

'Will you stop talking and let me finish? What I was going to say was I've decided to stay.'

Joe swung her round and round until they collapsed against the side of the caravan. They kissed each other delight-edly and then sat on the steps with their arms around each other.

'Now, Joe Baines, it's time I cleared up the mess in my home.'

'I'll come in and help. We'll have it done in no time, but first I'm going to phone to arrange to get the lock on the door fixed so that you'll feel safe tonight.'

It turned out to be fun putting things away with Joe for company. Most of the time they chatted, but occasionally he burst into song and she joined in. The locksmith arrived and fixed the door.

Joe carefully hung the last of her clothes in the cupboard and surveyed the room. 'It probably hasn't been quite as tidy as this since you moved in,' he quipped.

'Cheek, but thanks for your help. Shouldn't you be at work?'

'Yes, I'd better go. Are you sure you're going to be all right?'

'I'll be fine. I'm going to have something delicious to eat now.'

'Beans on toast?'

'How did you guess?' They shared another cuddle before Joe let himself out of the caravan, a big soppy grin on his face.

Ellie was feeling ready for the two slices of toast with steaming hot beans she'd set on the table, but just as she was about to start eating there was a knock on the door. She debated whether or not to answer it, but then called out, 'Come in, the door's unlocked.'

It was Owen. He was wearing khaki skinny chinos, topped with a block-stripe short-sleeved shirt, and looked slightly more tanned than last time she'd seen him. Once again she thought how attractive he was, if a little flashy.

'Mind if I join you?'

'You can make a pot of tea before you sit down. There's bread you can toast, if you like.'

'I brought wine.' He produced a bottle from the plastic bag he was holding. 'I'm afraid I went for a screw top as I wasn't sure if you'd have a bottle opener here.'

There was something about his condescending attitude which annoyed her. 'I do have one and I also have glasses if you want to get a couple out. In that cupboard there.' She decided she'd carry on and not let her meal get cold. She'd offered him toast and he could help himself. It was up to him.

Owen sat down and poured two glasses of wine. He raised his. 'Cheers.'

'Not bad,' she said after taking a sip, 'Although I preferred the champagne at Joe's opening night. Were you there?'

'Baines didn't invite me. But I did hear about your little accident.'

'Everyone knows everything here, don't they? I expect you've heard about that awful developer wanting to ruin this caravan site. The locals would be a lot happier if he went a long way away.'

Owen frowned. 'Let's not talk about him. I want to know about you.'

Ellie was surprised to find Owen was good company and they were soon

197

chatting and laughing, although Ellie couldn't help but compare him with Joe. Somehow Joe was open and honest in contrast to Owen's detachment. She'd admit that most women would find Owen more attractive, but when she thought of Joe a happy glow filled her. And another positive was that Owen wasn't being as pushy as he had been previously. He didn't mention going out.

'Thanks, Ellie. Sorry I barged in unexpectedly. To be honest I was concerned when I heard about your fall and the steps. I wanted to make sure you were all right. I know Baines is busy at the moment so will be leaving you to yourself.'

'I've enjoyed the evening. Thank you, Owen. Come again. Any time.'

He smiled and left.

First impressions weren't always right, she thought. She'd been wrong about Phyllis and wrong about Owen. He was a very nice man and good company. She couldn't help but wonder why he had bothered with her this evening when he could probably have had his pick of young women for company. It was very strange, but Ellie was happy to have someone else in the town she could think of as a potential friend. Her thoughts turned to Joe. She wouldn't tell him Owen had spent the evening with her because she sensed he'd be unhappy and it wasn't any of his business anyway.

⋆ ⋆ ⋆

Ellie hadn't seen Phyllis for a few days and she felt as though her other friends had disappeared completely. They weren't even coming into the shop for their groceries. Joe had rushed in a couple of times, but had been too busy to stop.

She was feeling miserable and the only time she'd felt happy was when Owen had called into the shop and made her feel good when he'd complimented her. She knew he was smooth and didn't mean half what he said, but she needed the boost. She was determined that after work she'd set off to see Phyllis and find out what it was she'd done wrong, if anything.

Phyllis didn't look too happy when she saw who her visitor was. 'Oh, Ellie, I'm rather busy. Would you pop back another day?'

'No, Phyllis, I won't. I'm fed up with everyone avoiding me. If I've offended someone I want to know what it is I've done. It's not right to just ignore me.' It crossed her mind that someone could have found out Owen had visited her at the caravan. She had the impression he wasn't well liked.

Phyllis relented. 'You're right, dear. Come into the kitchen and I'll put the kettle on.'

Ellie knew better than to offer to do it for her, but it was difficult to sit still and watch her struggle. She had to hand it to Phyllis: she was certainly a fighter. No sitting on the sidelines for her.

'There we are, dear. I've used mugs. As you said, they're easier to carry than cups and saucers. Have a slice of cake.' She pushed the plate over. 'Gwyneth and Vanessa arrived yesterday and we had a lovely time in the kitchen. The freezer's full of delicious cakes now. Tommy's been to visit of course.'

'So what's troubling everyone? Why is no one being friendly to me?'

'We've been avoiding you because we didn't want to tell you what Tommy saw one evening last week. I wish I wasn't the one to have to hurt you.'

'Go on.'

'I'm afraid this is going to be painful, dear. He was on duty for that open-air concert on the green. And he saw Joe when they were all leaving at the end.'

'That's right. Joe told me he was going with Amber. He said there were some good bands.'

'I see. Then maybe I don't need to tell you the rest.'

'Which is?'

'Tommy said they were behaving like

a couple. Arms round each other, laughing. In Tommy's words it looked as though they were out on a date.'

Ellie couldn't speak at first. So that was why Joe hadn't been very friendly. He'd finally succumbed to Amber's tenacity. Anger bubbled up inside her. He could have told her so that she knew where she stood. He'd just left her hanging on, waiting. He wasn't the man she'd thought. She stood up. 'I'm off.'

'I thought you might stay and have something to eat with me.'

'Another time. I need to make a phone call.'

* * *

Back at the caravan Ellie searched for the piece of paper on which Owen had written his number and called him.

'Ellie here. How about that date?' Joe had tried to warn her off Owen, but she'd decide for herself. And she no longer cared for Joe's opinion.

When Ellie drove to the next town to

meet Owen, she was pleased to be out of Fairsands. The town she'd grown to love over so short a time had become stifling. She parked the car and walked to the market square as instructed by Owen. He gave a brief wave and came over to her.

After a quick peck on the cheek he took her arm possessively and they walked towards a brash-looking pub. Ellie was surprised as she thought Owen would have preferred something more traditional. Inside everything was bright lights and piped music, which she didn't like. It was a bit like the pubs she'd been to with her friends from the flat, but that life seemed so long ago now. She glanced around uneasily. 'Have you been here before?' she asked Owen.

'Several times.' He laughed and greeted a group of people near the door like old friends. 'In fact, I own it.'

'You do?' Ellie was amazed. She hadn't considered Owen being a pub owner; she hadn't given a thought as to what his job might be.

'That and many others around here,' he replied. 'There's a lot you don't know about me, Ellie. Come on, let's sit down and get to know each other.'

Ellie felt uneasy now and wondered if she could make excuses and leave, but then she remembered Joe and Amber. Despair welled inside her; why was she so keen to get her own back? Joe probably wouldn't even care that she was out with Owen and it was wrong to use Owen as a scapegoat. 'I don't know if I should be here,' she started. 'I only wanted . . . '

'Shush,' whispered Owen. 'We're out to enjoy ourselves. I'm sure we'll have a great time. We'll have a drink and then go through to the restaurant. I think you'll be surprised; it's not a bit like the one Joe Baines saw fit to open in Fairsands.'

'Did I hear you mention Fairsands?' called a man who appeared beside them. He laughed and winked broadly at Owen. 'Aren't you going to introduce me?'

For the next half an hour or so, Ellie was surrounded by Owen's friends. She knew nothing about what they were discussing or the people they mentioned. At one time she thought she heard the name Phyllis Dewar, but she could have been imagining that. She sat politely sipping her orange juice and waited for Owen to remember they were supposed to be getting to know each other. This wasn't the sort of date she'd imagined. It was her own fault, she reflected; she'd set it up out of spite.

Just as she was about to make her apologies and leave, Owen said, 'Now, if you'll excuse us, Ellie and I are going to the restaurant. I'll catch up with you all later in the week.' He turned to her and gave a wide beam, standing up and taking her drink. They went into the restaurant and were seated in a cosy corner overlooking a little courtyard. 'We can eat outside if you'd like to, but it might get chilly later on.'

'This is fine,' said Ellie, glad they were alone. 'It's quieter in here.'

'I'm afraid so. Do you mind?'

'I love it. I've got used to the quiet in Fairsands.'

'I find it dead, especially for young-sters. There's nothing to do. It's all right for people like Phyllis and her cronies, but some people want a bit of action.'

'Like an amusement arcade, you mean?' Ellie didn't want to discuss it, but thought it might be worth a mention to find out which side Owen had been on. As if she couldn't guess.

He raised his eyebrows. 'That's exactly what I mean. You know then. About me?'

'What about you?' Ellie was mysti-fied.

'I'm the one who started up the campaign for the amusement arcade in Fairsands. You must have heard about it. Didn't anyone tell you it was me?'

Ellie shook her head silently. She couldn't take this in. Did Phyllis and

Joe think she knew about Owen and the amusement arcade? Phyllis was probably so wrapped up with her crusade against it, that she couldn't conceive anyone not knowing it was Owen who was involved. She'd warned Ellie about him, but hadn't explained why. Joe had also tried to put her off. Now she understood.

Realising her mouth had dropped open, Ellie quickly closed it and tried to think of a suitable reply. 'I had no idea,' she said at length. 'I knew about the plan, of course, but I didn't know it was your project.' They sat in silence.

Owen reached for her hand and gripped it. 'Please don't walk out. I thought you knew about it. Will you stay and have dinner?' He raised her hand to his lips and said, 'You invited me out, remember?'

Ellie felt her cheeks grow hot. He was right; she had asked him to take her out and here she was caught up in a web from which she would find it hard to disentangle herself. 'All right,' she sighed. 'I'll stay, but please, we are not to discuss anything to do with your plans in Fairsands.'

'Suits me,' said Owen. He handed her a menu. 'I recommend the lobster.'

After the air had been cleared, Ellie relaxed and found herself chatting easily again to Owen. Despite the brashness of the pub, the meal was good, although she couldn't help comparing it with Joe's restaurant food which had been superb. Thinking about Joe made her sad. She decided she'd get in touch with him when she returned home.

Owen waved her off and went back inside. Ellie was pleased she'd come in her own car and not let Owen bring her. On the short journey home, she reflected on the fact of Owen being the property developer everyone was so much against. She could understand their prejudices, but he hadn't won his fight; nor had he given in gracefully, she acknowledged. Was he biding his time before he dropped the next bombshell?

11

More and more, Ellie found herself wanting to get in touch with Joe. She couldn't believe he'd betrayed her and lied about his relationship with Amber. Although she didn't doubt Phyllis's or her other friends' intentions, she knew Joe to be honest and upfront about things. As she let herself into the caravan, she stifled a yawn. It was probably not the best time to ring Joe; she was tired and he would be busy at the restaurant. Besides, she had work in the morning. Hopefully, people would no longer be avoiding her in the shop.

When Ellie fell into bed, she slept immediately and only woke when her alarm and the birds wakened her. It was another beautiful summer's day and she showered and dressed, humming to herself. She'd got over last night being a mistake and now viewed it as provident.

She understood a bit more about what Phyllis and Joe had intimated about Owen.

During her mid-morning break at work, Ellie stepped out of the shop and phoned Joe. He answered on the second ring, but his reply was a curt, 'I can't talk at the moment. I'll ring you back.'

Ellie stared at the phone in dismay; she'd never known Joe like that. Tears pricked her eyes, but she wouldn't let them flow. Instead she phoned Phyllis and said she'd be over when the shop shut. At least Phyllis was pleased to hear her and wanted to see her.

★ ★ ★

'You did what?' Phyllis was outraged. 'After all we said? You went out with Owen? When you didn't have to?'

'Calm down, Phyllis. It was only a meal. Anyway, he told me how he was involved with the amusement arcade and why you're all so against him. He was understanding about your opinion of him.'

Phyllis shook her head. 'I don't want to talk about Owen Wilde. Tell me about Joe. Does he know you've been out with Owen?'

Ellie frowned. 'I tried to ring him, but he was distant. He wouldn't speak to me.'

'He's a lot on his plate at the moment, if you'll excuse the pun,' smiled Phyllis. 'Oh, Ellie, what are we going to do with you? You and Joe are made for each other, but you don't seem to realise it.'

'I thought we'd come to a bit of an understanding,' admitted Ellie. 'But if he's given up on me and gone back to Amber, there's nothing I can do about it.' Ellie didn't like the gleam in Phyllis's eyes. 'And you're not to interfere,' she admonished her before grinning. 'Are you always such a matchmaker?'

'Only with people I like.' They sat in the sitting room and Ellie thought back to the time she'd spent there when she first arrived at Fairsands. 'How's your arm, Phyllis? You never complain about it. It must be a frightful nuisance for you.'

'I've been through worse. Anyway, it's only a couple more weeks before the plaster comes off.'

A crash made them both jump. Ellie was on her feet and into the kitchen, heading for the back door. She wrenched it open and came face to face with Amber. 'What do you think you're doing?'

Phyllis was at the back door now and Ellie tried to shield her in case Amber was there to wreak more havoc. But to her surprise, Amber buried her head in her hands and her shoulders heaved as she sobbed long and hard. Ellie looked at Phyllis and raised her arms helplessly. They waited for Amber to bring herself under control. Knowing Phyllis didn't really want the young woman in her house, Ellie gestured for Phyllis to go back in and shut the door, which she did.

'What's the matter, Amber? Afraid you've been found out? What were you about to do this time?' Ellie kept her voice stern, although she sensed there wouldn't be a fight. 'Come on, I'll walk you home,' offered Ellie, knowing she only lived around the corner.

At Amber's front door a familiar figure loomed. Of course it was Joe. Ellie didn't know whether she was pleased to see him or frustrated that he was at Amber's house. At that moment, she felt as if all the stuffing had been knocked out of her.

'Can we come in, Amber?' asked Joe. 'I think the three of us need to talk, don't you?'

Amber sniffed and nodded, unlocking the door and going inside. In the sitting room, Amber said, 'Sit down both of you. You're right, Joe, we need to clear the air. I'm not happy going on like this. I didn't want to get involved, but he made me. He convinced me you'd want to be my boyfriend, Joe. It's all I've ever wanted.'

Ellie felt most uncomfortable and made to leave. 'No,' said Joe. 'I've a feeling Amber wants to speak to us both.'

Amber swallowed hard. She didn't look either of them in the eye as she said, 'I broke the pots at Phyllis's house and smashed the cake in the kitchen. It was a stupid thing to do. I thought it would scare you and send you home, Ellie.'

'But why would you want Ellie to go? At that time, she was only here for a few days to look after Phyllis.'

Amber shrugged. 'I wanted Ellie to go so that you and I could get back together, Joe. Look, Joe, I'm sorry, all right?' She turned a watery half-smile to Ellie. 'Can we forget it now?'

As she was about to agree, Joe almost shouted, 'Forget it? Of course we can't. What about Ellie's caravan home? And who is *he*?'

'You want to blame me for every-thing, don't you, Joe? Well, it's not my fault. How could I know what happened in her caravan?'

Something about her shifty look told Ellie that Amber knew more than she was letting on, but she wasn't going to tackle her about it now. She must have been prompted by mere jealousy. That was something Ellie could understand; she'd been jealous of Amber when she'd heard that she and Joe had been out together. 'I'm going home now,' she said. 'You do what you want to, Joe.'

Having called on Phyllis to fill her in on the latest from Amber, Ellie went back to the caravan. Phyllis wasn't pleased with her on two counts: the fact that she'd been out with Owen, and that she insisted on staying at the caravan. Ellie had tried to reassure her that Amber was no longer a threat, but Ellie admitted to herself that if Amber hadn't messed up her things at the caravan, then someone else had to be responsible. This move to Fairsands was turning out to be quite an adventure, some of which Ellie was enjoying and some of which was worrying her.

To her surprise, just as she was about to get ready for bed, someone knocked on her door. 'Joe? Come in. What's happened?'

'I wanted to see you,' said Joe, but he wasn't his usual happy self. This Joe looked disheartened. More than anything, Ellie wanted to comfort him, but wasn't sure if her arms around him would be welcomed now. He'd been quite distant recently. 'You must know now that there's nothing between Amber and me.'

It wasn't quite phrased as a question, but Ellie said, 'I believe you, Joe, but what were you doing at Amber's house when we turned up there?'

'I'd come to tell her she was making things difficult for us. I didn't want to be unkind. What I want is for you and me to be together and I was going to tell her.'

'I think it was good to clear the air with her. But almost everyone saw you with her at the concert and thought . . . '

'I can imagine what they thought,' said Joe. 'So the gossip got back to you, did it?' He ran his fingers through his hair. 'I told you she had tickets. I saw it as an opportunity to find out whether or not she was responsible for the incidents. She didn't say a word about them. I wasn't hiding anything. It was very crowded and she hung onto me. What was I supposed to do? Tell her to back off in case rumours got back to you? Anyway,' he continued, colour rising in his cheeks, 'you can talk. You haven't been completely straight with me, have you?'

'Whatever do you mean?' Ellie was puzzled.

'Rumours got back to me as well. About you and Wilde. How could you, Ellie? I warned you he wasn't trustworthy.' Joe gave a sigh. 'Sorry, it's nothing to do with me who you see. I just thought . . . hoped . . . ' He trailed off.

'Oh, Joe, everything's getting out of proportion, isn't it? Sit down and I'll make some hot chocolate. That's if you can spare the time.'

Then Joe grinned and his face lit up. 'I'd like that, Ellie. I know I haven't been in touch with you much lately, but I've had, well, a lot to think about what with the shop, the restaurant and . . . you.'

That made Ellie happier. 'Going out with Owen was a mistake. If I'm honest, I was trying to get back at you for seeing Amber. It was a silly thing to do and it won't happen again. He's not my type. He's good-looking, but I'm not keen on the false tan and gold chain.' She stirred the drinks and handed a mug to Joe, sitting beside him on the bench seat by the window. 'Let's treat ourselves to a bit of relaxation, shall we?'

They sat together and sipped their drinks. Ellie was pleased they were back on a level base again. She'd missed the closeness which had been growing between them. Perhaps now that the spectre of Amber was out of the way, they'd be able to move forward and get to know each other better without any obstacles.

Joe placed his cup on the table and put his arm around Ellie. She rested her head on his shoulder and enjoyed his nearness.

A bit later, although she didn't want to spoil their time together, she knew they both needed to sleep. Joe hadn't said a word and when she disentangled herself from his arm, he snored softly and almost fell into her lap. He'd been asleep all the time! Ellie smiled, pleased he'd been relaxed enough to do that.

Gently she shook him. 'Time for bed.'

Joe snuffled awake and stared at her. 'How long have I been asleep?' he mumbled. 'Oh, Ellie, I'm sorry. This isn't very romantic of me, is it?'

'It's nice to have you here. But we both have work tomorrow and we need some rest.'

Joe struggled to his feet and blinked. Then he cupped her face in his hands and kissed her nose. 'You're a very

lovely person. I'm glad we're friends.'
And then he left.

Ellie never thought she'd get to sleep
as she lay awake thinking about Joe.
Things were back on with him and the
future looked rosy.

* * *

'Ellie, I'm pleased you're here,' said
Jane as she darted to and fro in the
shop. 'One of the paperboys hasn't
turned up. Joe hadn't planned to come
in this morning and I can only stay for
a couple of hours. What shall we do?'

Thinking rapidly, Ellie said, 'You
hold the fort here; I'll deliver the papers
which haven't gone out. Could you get
in touch with Gwyneth? Would she
come in today?'

'You're a lifesaver,' said Jane. 'Now I
see why Joe hired you.'

Ellie picked up the loaded bag, glad
her ankle was well and truly healed
now, and set off to deliver the papers.
She'd only done them a couple of

times, but she remembered the route and got them distributed promptly.

'Gwyneth's coming in at ten,' smiled Jane. She lowered her voice as a customer entered the shop. 'My other job is much better paid than this one. It's not Joe's fault, or his parents', but Mick and I need the money, as I explained to you.'

'Jane, is it Owen Wilde you work for?' Ellie was quite sure the developer Jane had been talking about was Owen, but she wanted to be certain.

'Yes. He seems quite nice, really. I know there was a lot of bad feeling when he wanted to introduce an amusement arcade to Fairsands, but he seems to be a fair man to work for.'

'And he *is* good-looking,' smiled Ellie in order to lighten the mood.

'Oh yes, you're right, he is.' Jane giggled and then went behind the counter to serve the customer.

During the afternoon, Joe came into the shop. 'Hello, Ellie, Gwyneth,' he greeted them. 'Thank you for helping out. We've a great little team here, although Jane won't be working with us for much longer. Gwyneth, I was hoping you might consider coming in on a more permanent basis. Would you do that?'

'For you, Joe, anything,' said Gwyneth, a big smile on her face. 'Really, I mean it. I love being here. And Ellie's such fun to work with. I'm not so sure about going on the paper rounds, though.'

'Oh, I don't mind doing those,' put in Ellie. 'The exercise does me good.'

'Can I have a private word, Ellie?' asked Joe. They moved to the back of the shop. 'Will you meet me for a drink later? Perhaps you could come to the restaurant — would that be all right?'

'Sure, Joe. Is something up? You look a bit anxious.'

Joe shook his head. 'Everything's fine. Just got too many things to think about. Never mind, Mum and Dad will be back at some stage and I've got a very efficient shop manager until then. I'll be sorry to lose Jane — she knows the customers, the delivery men, the paper people . . . Still, nothing stays the same.'

12

Stacking shelves in the shop gave Ellie time to think about Joe's words. When his parents came back she would be superfluous again, but worse than that: jobless and homeless. She must find out when they were due to return and start making plans. The thought of having to move away was almost unbearable.

Joe was busy in the restaurant kitchen when she arrived. 'Help yourself to a drink and I'll be with you in a minute,' he said.

Ellie walked to the bar and surveyed the bottles before selecting a carton of juice from a fridge. She found a glass and settled herself on one of the bar stools. When Joe joined her and kissed her all the worries melted away.

'I'm beginning to wonder if I've taken on more than I can manage. There aren't enough hours in the day to get everything done.'

Ellie had already noticed he had dark circles under his eyes and was looking slightly dishevelled. 'You don't need to worry about the shop. Everything is going smoothly and I promise I'll let you know if we have any problems.'

'That's a relief.'

'But I've been thinking. When your mum and dad come back I won't be needed, will I?'

'Needed? You most definitely *will* be needed.' He took hold of her hand and squeezed it. 'I'll always need you.'

'Be serious, Joe. I mean at the shop.' Although she batted aside Joe's comment, she was pleased to hear the words he spoke.

'Don't worry about that. I've been in constant contact with Mum and Dad and they've made the decision to semi-retire. They'll still oversee the management of the shop and the caravans, but they don't want to be hands-on anymore. I've suggested they might like to consider you as the permanent shop manager.'

'I'll have to look for somewhere else to live if they decide to take me on.'

'I've been thinking about that too. I'm not happy about you being at the caravan. If Amber didn't do those things — and I think we both believe she didn't — then who did, and why? I feel you're vulnerable there.'

'I'm perfectly happy at the caravan, but I do realise I can't stay there forever.' Ellie wasn't sure she even *wanted* to stay there. After her caravan had been messed up, it hadn't felt like the cosy home she'd grown fond of. She still wasn't convinced Amber hadn't been responsible and a little bit of her was disgruntled at the thought of Joe believing Amber to be blameless.

'You wouldn't consider living in the flat above here for a while, would you?' Joe asked. 'It's just about ready.'

'That's where you're going to live.'

'It is. But I'd stay at Mum and Dad's

until you've found somewhere else, or . . .'

'Or what?'

Joe looked sheepish. 'Nothing.'

Neither of them spoke for a while.

'There's something else I want to talk to you about.' Joe frowned. 'It's Jane. I can't understand why she's leaving.'

'I think she likes accounts and the job she's been offered is also better paid.'

'The thing is, she's being a bit odd with me, and when I asked who she was going to work for she looked embarrassed and changed the subject. I'm pretty sure you know what's going on.'

'I do.' Ellie sipped her drink.

'And you're going to tell me?'

'No, I'm not. She told me in confidence so I'm afraid I can't tell you anything except what's common knowledge. You must already know that Jane and Mick are struggling financially and by changing jobs Jane thinks they'll be able to manage. She *is* embarrassed about leaving the shop and going to work for someone else. I doubt we'll see much of her.'

Joe extended his arms and enveloped Ellie in a bear hug, nearly spilling her drink. 'Your loyalty is commendable,' he whispered. Pulling away, he added, 'It doesn't stop me from wondering, though.'

Ellie smiled. 'Why don't you ask Jane?'

'I might just do that. Anyway, I didn't invite you here to gossip about co-workers.'

'And what *did* you invite me here for?' asked Ellie, hoping it wasn't to ask her to do the early-morning paper round.

'So that I could enjoy your company. We haven't had a lot of time alone, have we, Ellie? You must know I'm fond of you. Do you think we could spend more time together?'

Her heart leapt. This was what she had longed for. More than anything, she wanted to spend time with Joe Baines. He had ensnared her from when they first met. She smiled what she hoped was an encouraging smile. To her surprise, he turned his back and got on with ticking things off a list on the work counter. Then, still with his back to her, he started singing another tender love song.

Ellie gulped her drink, not daring to look at him, not daring not to. All she could see was the back of his neck, which looked so vulnerable she wanted to reach out and stroke it. Since she'd known Joe, she'd discovered another side to herself — one she'd never thought possible. And the best thing was, she liked it!

She prepared to be entertained. He certainly had an amazing voice. Relaxing into a reverie, she didn't take notice of the fact that she was joining in with him. Immediately Joe was by her side, smiling into her eyes, and they sang in unison. When the last note died away, Ellie wished she'd died with it. That was truly embarrassing, as she knew her voice was like a distress signal.

Joe kissed the top of her head. 'That was nice,' he said. 'I didn't know singing was among your list of attributes.'

Feeling her face was the colour of a boiled lobster, Ellie let out a breath. 'I'd prefer it if you didn't spread the word. Sorry, I got carried away.'

'You've a lovely voice, Ellie.' Joe frowned. 'Natural, soft and sweet. Just like the rest of you, in fact.' He bounded around putting things away, wiping surfaces down and generally being busy. Ellie thought he'd forgotten she was there, but then he was by her side again. 'Right, that's work finished for now. Fancy a stroll by the sea?'

She loved the sea. The fresh air would cool her down, but Joe's presence wouldn't, she decided. In those few short moments with him, she knew that they had become closer than before.

'The hours you work are very erratic, Joe. Will you be able to keep it up?'

'I've got to, Ellie. The restaurant is my dream come true. I must make a success of it. And I promised Mum and Dad I'd look after the shop. It won't be for much longer that I've got to do the two things together.' He put an arm around her shoulder. 'That's why it means so much to me that you're here. You're a great help and I can relax with you in the driving seat at the shop.'

'Is that why you want me here? Is that it?' Ellie was disappointed he hadn't said he wanted her there for himself.

'Now who's fishing for compliments?' Joe laughed. 'I love having you here, Ellie. I just wish we had more time to get to know each other. Bringing you out to the beach at the dead of night is . . . well, it's sort of romantic, I suppose, but it would be nice to do a few more normal things.'

'Like going out for a meal, the cinema, that sort of thing? If that's what you mean, then let me say that I'm more than happy to be strolling along the seafront with you.' Glad of the darkness, Ellie could feel her face growing warm again. She didn't want to look at him. Deciding to change the subject, she asked, 'Where do you get your fish? It must be local.'

'Oh I get up early and go fishing myself. It's my hobby.'

'Really?' Ellie was amazed.

A low chuckle followed by, 'No, not really,' had her swiping at him. He let her go and raced along the beach, Ellie in hot pursuit. He must have slowed, she reflected, as she caught him up easily. When she was level, Joe turned and held out his arms to her. She cannoned into them and he wrapped her in a big hug from which she never wanted to escape.

Eventually Joe released her and took her hand. 'I suppose we should go back. It's been great, Ellie. Thanks for coming over. Can we do it again sometime?'

She put her head on his shoulder and nuzzled into him. 'That would be nice.' Then she yawned and let him lead her towards home.

It was crazy, but each time Ellie

neared her caravan home, she felt slightly uneasy despite what she had said. He'd wanted to take her right to the door, but Ellie shooed him off as he looked shattered. Now she wished she'd let him bring her the extra distance. If Amber hadn't been responsible for the two incidents at the caravan, who had? Then she remembered Amber had mentioned *he*. Joe had asked her who it was, but Amber had been so distraught, she hadn't answered his question. Perhaps it was time to ask her again. But not now. Now, Ellie wanted to get to bed as the working day was fast approaching.

As she got ready to sleep, Ellie mulled over what Joe had said about her moving into the flat over the restaurant. It would be a perfect solution. Or would it? Being that accessible to Joe might not be such a good idea. With her head on the pillow and a silly grin on her face, she knew that she was definitely in love with him. And she had a feeling he felt the same about her. How long would she have to wait to hear him declare it?

With those thoughts, she buried her head in her pillow and closed her eyes.

★ ★ ★

'Hello, it's me,' Ellie called as she rapped on the front door of Phyllis's house. The door opened almost immediately. 'I looked through the records and saw it was about time for Ludo's tins of food to be delivered.'

'It's a good job you were paying attention. I'd completely forgotten to keep tabs on it. Look, Ludo, what's Ellie brought you?' The old dog looked up from the rug by Phyllis's chair, grunted and plopped his head on his paws again.

'Obviously Ludo appreciates me,' joked Ellie, carrying the carton through to the kitchen. 'Shall I put a few tins in the cupboard and the rest in the shed?'

Having done that, she settled down with Phyllis, who had made tea.

Lifting her cup, Ellie said, 'You used to prefer coffee if I remember correctly.'

Phyllis shrugged her shoulders. 'Everyone else seems to make tea when they come here. If you can't beat 'em, join 'em, I say. Anyway, that tea Joe's got in on special offer isn't too bad.'

'I'll pass on the compliment, shall I?'

'Talking of Joe . . . ' Phyllis's eyes gleamed, which told Ellie she was expecting more gossip.

'We weren't, were we? I was wondering how you're getting to your hospital appointment. Is anyone free to take you?'

'Gwyneth was going to, but I think Joe wants her to work more hours, doesn't he? Vanessa's busy. I'm not having Amber come with me even if she offers. I'll be all right; I can get a taxi.'

'I'll ask Joe for time off. Perhaps I can re-arrange my half-day. You're not going on your own.' Thankfully, Phyllis put up no opposition. Ellie finished her tea, washed the mugs and went out to her car. 'See you again soon. Take care.'

But Ellie didn't go straight back to the shop. She turned up the next street and parked outside Amber's house. There were questions she wanted answers to. There was no reply when she banged on the front door, but just as she was about to walk away, there was a movement in an upstairs window; a net curtain flapped and Ellie was sure it wasn't caused by the breeze. Rapidly, she banged on the door again and stood back looking up at the bedroom.

At last there was the sound of footsteps and the door opened a fraction. 'What do you want?' asked Amber.

'To talk to you, that's all. May I come in? I'm sure you don't want your neighbours to hear what I've got to say.' As she hoped, Amber stood aside and let Ellie in.

They stood awkwardly in the hallway. Amber didn't invite Ellie into the sitting room, but she closed the front door firmly.

'When Joe and I spoke to you, you

indicated someone encouraged you to do those things you did at Phyllis's house. I'd like to know who *he* is. Can't you tell me, Amber?'

The woman facing Ellie looked pale and was shaking. 'What does it matter? I won't do anything else. Please don't tell Tommy.' Amber's eyes filled with tears. 'It's all right for you. Joe thinks the world of you, everyone knows that. Even *I* accept it now. It was hard at first, but now I've got a bit of a chance of happiness which could so easily be snatched away if . . . the person you're referring to finds out I told you who he is.'

So, that confirmed there was someone else involved. It seemed unfair to press Amber further right then. She was so vulnerable. Ellie hoped things would turn out all right for her, and told her so. She was rewarded with a gentle pressure on her arm and the beginnings of a smile.

'You're nice, Ellie. Joe deserves you. I hope you'll both be happy together.'

Ellie returned to the shop pleased she'd followed her instinct and visited Amber. Perhaps it didn't matter too much who else had been involved. Nothing sinister had happened lately. She was surprised to see Joe behind the counter.

'Gwyneth said you'd delivered Ludo's food, Ellie. I could have done that. Deliveries aren't part of your job description.'

'I was happy to help out and I don't mind doing other orders. I like the variety.'

Joe ran his fingers through his hair. 'Is there anything you won't do, Ellie?'

She put her head on one side, considering. 'As long as it's legal, I'll give it a go.'

Gwyneth said, 'Jane came in soon after you left, Ellie. I haven't had time to tell Joe, but she wants to speak to us all about something. She's coming again at about four, as she thought that would be the most convenient time to get us all together. Anyone have any idea what it's about?'

Ellie and Joe exchanged looks, but neither said anything. Dead on four o'clock, Jane arrived. The shop was fairly busy with school children crowding in to buy crisps and chocolate to see them home after a hard day's learning. When the rush had died down, Jane's friends gathered around her, eager to hear what she had to say.

Taking a deep breath, she started. 'I'm sorry to be leaving, as I've enjoyed working here with you all. Thank you for putting up with me, but I won't be far away and will pop in as a customer. As you're all aware, I cut my hours, but not all of you know the reason why.' She glanced at Ellie, who smiled encouragingly. 'I'd like to finish here completely on Friday, if that's all right, Joe. And then . . . well, then I'll be working in the accounts department of Owen Wilde's offices over by the bank in the high street. His previous accounts clerk has left.' She paused and licked her lips, looking at them all as if expecting to be sentenced to the guillotine for being a turncoat.

Joe gave Jane a hug and said, 'We're sorry to lose you, Jane. You've been a wonderful person to have around. You have the answers to everything. And now we know where to find you, we can get in touch and ask if we're stuck.'

Ellie was amazed that he didn't flinch or say a word about Owen. He had said just the right things to make Jane feel comfortable and at ease.

'Hear, hear,' smiled Gwyneth. 'All the best to you, Jane. I hope you'll be very happy in your new job.'

As Jane left the shop with a happy smile on her face, Joe whispered to Ellie, 'Shall we meet again this evening? After the restaurant closes?'

'I'd love to.'

★   ★   ★

Ellie was ready, dressed in linen trousers and a light top, for another walk along the beach. She grabbed a fleece, as the late evening could be a bit chilly by the sea. Out of habit, she hesitated and checked the steps as she exited the caravan. A voice startled her.

'Ellie, how are things?'

She peered into the darkness. 'Owen? Whatever are you doing here?'

'Just passing,' he said. That surprised Ellie. Why would he be passing through the caravan park? As if reading her mind, he pointed. 'There's a short cut to the beach. I've only just finished work and I need to unwind or I'll never sleep.'

'I'm pleased you've taken Jane on. She's a good worker, but you must know that. How's business? The pub we went to certainly seemed to have plenty of customers. And I guess you're doing all right if you're taking on extra people.' Ellie wasn't that interested in what Owen was up to, but she wanted to be polite.

'It's nice you're interested. I know I'm not flavour of the month, or year come to that, but I'm not totally evil.' He flashed Ellie a smile and jogged off towards the lane.

With a shake of her head, Ellie tried to put aside thoughts that Owen could have been the one who messed up her stuff in the caravan and moved the steps. It was unthinkable. Owen might not be her idea of a knight in shining armour, but what could he hope to gain from perpetrating those kinds of actions?

This time, Joe was nearly ready when Ellie arrived. He kissed her cheek and directed her to a stool. Within a couple of minutes, everything was spick and span and the two set off in the direction of the seafront, hand in hand.

A crescent moon sat prettily in the indigo sky and bright stars shone. Everywhere was eerily quiet, something Ellie had embraced since coming to this remote part of the country. Abruptly, that silence was interrupted and she heard voices. Joe grasped her hand tightly and gestured for her to stop. Together they listened.

It wasn't unreasonable that other

people should be out at that time of night, but when Ellie recognised the voices, she became alert. It was Owen and Amber! She watched from the cover of darkness as Owen and Amber embraced. So that was the person Amber hoped she'd have a chance of happiness with. Things fitted into place. Ellie whipped her head up to look at Joe. From the look on his face, similar thoughts were flitting through his mind. Slowly, Joe turned Ellie round and they headed back the way they'd come, veering off at the short cut to the caravan.

'Is it all right if we go to your place, Ellie?' Joe whispered.

Sitting in the caravan sipping lemonade, they raised their eyebrows at each other.

'Well,' said Ellie, 'what did you make of that? Did you know that Amber was interested in Owen?'

'To be honest, I wish her well. I'm just glad she's out of my hair. And I'm glad he's not going to ask you out again. What I don't understand is why.'

'Perhaps they like each other, Joe. Had you thought of that? Often the simplest of reasons is the right one.'

'I still don't trust Wilde.' Joe sat looking glum. 'I don't begrudge him and Amber happiness, but I don't like to think of her — or anyone — being used in some game he's playing.'

'Let's talk about something else.' Ellie felt she was being a bit selfish, but she wanted to make the most of her time with Joe. Discussing Amber wasn't part of that plan.

'Like us, you mean? I'm happy to do that. Tell me what you would like your future to hold, Ellie.'

Oh no, I don't think so, thought Ellie. She didn't want to make a fool of herself by announcing her love for Joe — at least, not until she was sure it was reciprocated. Looking at Joe's open, honest face smiling at her, told her that he did feel the same. She hoped so. Aloud, she said, 'What you were saying about the flat above the restaurant?

Were you serious that I might be able to rent it to tide me over?'

'I'd love you to live there. This place gives me the creeps now I know how easy it is to damage. I don't want to risk your well-being for anything.' He put down his drink and leaned over towards Ellie, taking her hand. 'You've become very precious to me.' Then he lifted her hand to his soft mouth and kissed it. That simple gesture almost moved Ellie to tears. He really was very special himself.

13

'I've been to see Martha again and Wilde called on her recently and said if she didn't make her mind up soon he'd drop his offer,' Phyllis said to Ellie. The two were at the hospital waiting for Phyllis's plaster to be removed. 'She told him she'd make her mind up when she was good and ready, but between you and me I think she's already decided. She doesn't want to fall out with her friends so I'm pretty sure she won't sell to that young upstart. It's a huge relief. On the same subject, I had hoped to persuade you to move from that caravan by now, Ellie. You can move in with me if you like.'

'Phyllis Dewar,' called a white-coated young man.

'Over here,' replied Ellie, preparing to stand. She knew better than to try and help Phyllis, who was struggling to get off the unfamiliar hard plastic chair.

'He looks a bit too eager to me. Come with me, Ellie, and make sure he hasn't got a chainsaw in that little room.'

Ellie tried not to laugh outright as they huddled into the cubicle. The procedure was performed quickly and proficiently.

'All done,' said the plaster-room technician. 'Go easy with it; it's easy to overdo things.'

Phyllis arched an eyebrow at him. 'I have to get back to baking cakes as soon as possible,' she tried to explain, 'or the police will be after me.'

Ellie received a pitying look from the young man, but didn't bother to explain that Tommy was the police. 'Come on, Phyllis, let's get you home.'

In the car, Phyllis continued her interrogation. 'Well, will you move in with me?'

'Everyone's anxious to have me move in with them,' sighed Ellie, manoeuvring her way carefully among the busy streets near the hospital.

'Me and who else?'

'Joe . . . ' *Oh, Ellie*, she thought, *why did you say that?*

'Aha, I see.' Although Ellie kept her eyes on the road, she knew Phyllis's eyes would be twinkling and her mouth turning up in a smile.

'You don't, you know. He suggested I move into the flat above the restaurant.'

'Oh. Well it's a start, I suppose.'

Back at the house, Phyllis stared in dismay at her left arm. 'That looks pathetic,' she said. 'I thought I'd be able to carry on where I left off.'

Ellie's heart went out to the older woman. She'd been very positive while the plaster had been on, no doubt counting the days until it came off. 'Let's give it a wash and I'll put some cream on. It needs a bit of TLC.' *And so do you*, she thought. Poor Phyllis.

Later they sat with Phyllis peering at the leaflet the hospital had given her. 'Looks as if I was better off with the plaster on.' Tears glittered in her eyes and Ellie knew she was doing her best to maintain the indomitable front she always seemed to have.

'It takes time, Phyllis. Please don't get upset. We're all here to help you. You can have your groceries delivered and Ludo will still get his walks. And no doubt we can have an outing to Vanessa's café to celebrate your next step.'

Phyllis perked up. 'Next time, young lady, would you let Joe deliver Ludo's food, please? I may be old, but it's nice to have a handsome man fussing over me.' A beautiful smile lit her face. 'Now, make me a cup of something hot, would you, please? You're supposed to be looking after me, aren't you?'

* * *

'Come in, Ellie. I won't be long. We were busy earlier, but things have quietened down now.' Joe gave her a quick hug before going about his kitchen routine. Ellie was happy to sit and watch him work; he was very methodical and thorough. When she sensed he had nearly completed his tasks, she said, 'Can I have a look at the flat, please?'

Joe stopped what he was doing, holding a cloth in mid-air. 'You mean it? You've decided to leave the caravan? Oh, Ellie, I'm so relieved.'

'Don't get too excited; I only want to have a look. See if it's worth my while.' She enjoyed the easy way she could tease him.

'Go on up. I'll come in a few minutes.' Joe directed her to a side door in the corner of the kitchen she hadn't noticed before.

On closer inspection, Ellie found there was a separate entrance to the flat from the outside. She could be completely independent of the restaurant should she choose. She climbed the stairs to a front door definitely in need of a coat or two of paint. Putting that aside as a mere cosmetic job, she put her hand on the knob and turned the handle. She wished she hadn't conjured up a picture of a cosy little nest above Blue Horizon. The light she snapped on didn't help dispel the gloom inside. There were two rooms, a kitchen and a poky bathroom, she discovered. It didn't take long to explore them. Empty boxes and other debris lay around the dirty floor. The caravan was infinitely preferable to this tip.

'What do you think?' She hadn't heard Joe come in. He stood watching her, his face bright. Did he think he'd handed her Buckingham Palace on a plate?

'Well . . . it's a bit . . . ' What could she say that wouldn't dampen his enthusiasm?

'Putting aside any superficial decorating. Even I can see it needs a lick of paint.' He looked around and grimaced. 'Oh, Ellie, who am I kidding? If only I'd decorated it before showing it to you.'

'Don't worry, I've a good imagination,' she assured him. 'I can definitely see possibilities.' But at that moment, she couldn't think of any good ones.

'Let's leave it for a couple of days and return with a fresh outlook.' Joe was already backing out of the door. After one more glance around her, Ellie followed him, switching off the light as she went.

Downstairs, Joe asked, 'To the beach again? Your caravan? Or shall we just stay here? We can have a drink and a sandwich in the restaurant if you like.'

'Shall we stay here?' said Ellie. 'Fruit juice would be very welcome, but I'm not hungry.'

Joe frowned. 'I am.'

They went back to the restaurant and Joe pulled out a chair at a corner table for Ellie to sit down. Then he went to the large fridge and inspected the contents. 'Mango, pineapple, orange, apple . . . '

'Mango sounds good. Do you usually have exotic stuff lying around?' She didn't remember seeing those drinks when she was there before. Somehow she had imagined Joe would go for more traditional things. There was a lot she didn't know about him. She sipped her drink, watching him make a large, untidy sandwich filled with sliced meat and salad. 'Is that on the menu?'

Joe let out a rumble of laughter. 'Only my personal one. Can you picture a customer's face if I placed this in front of him?' With a sharp knife he cut the bread in half before taking a huge bite.

Then they both heard a noise. Ellie was about to groan, but made herself keep quiet. She desperately hoped it wasn't a re-run of the first time she'd been at the restaurant with Joe.

Still carrying his sandwich, Joe went to the door and yanked it open. 'Wilde! What are you doing skulking around my dustbins?'

'I saw the light and thought you'd like some company.' Owen appeared to answer easily and looked relaxed.

'I've already got some.' Joe gestured across to where Ellie was sitting.

'Thanks for your concern.'

Owen lifted a hand in an acknowledging gesture to Ellie. 'I'll be off then.'

Joe closed the door with a bang. 'Do you believe that? He's got a nerve coming round here at this time of night.'

Ellie put a hand on Joe's arm. 'Do you really think Owen was behind all the things that have happened?'

Joe took another bite of his sandwich and bobbed his head up and down. 'Oh yes, I'm almost sure of it. And you? What do you think?'

'I agree with you,' replied Ellie firmly. 'But why?'

'Because he didn't get what he wanted so he's making things hard for us. I wonder if we should talk to Amber again.' He put the rest of his sandwich down. 'Now. Let's go.'

'I think we should leave her in peace. She's vulnerable.'

'I'm going. It's up to you if you come with me or not.'

Ellie was surprised at his sudden eagerness and decided she should go with him.

* * *

The door opened a crack and Amber peered out. 'What do you want?'

'Some answers, that's all. Wouldn't that be the right thing to do, Amber? To tell us what's been going on.' Joe put his foot in the door so that it couldn't be closed on them. 'I know it's late, but this is important.'

'I don't want to upset Owen.'

'He won't know we've been. We just need some questions answered. Please, Amber.'

Amber opened the door wide and led them into the sitting room.

Ellie looked around at the luggage and piles of possessions dotted round the room. 'Are you going on holiday?'

'No. Look, I'll tell you everything if you promise not to tell Owen or the police. I've got the chance of a fresh start.' She glanced at her watch. 'Sit down if you can find somewhere and I'll tell you the whole story.'

Joe and Ellie perched on the edge of the settee and waited.

'I always liked you, Joe. I thought we made a good couple. When you broke up with me it was the most awful time, but then I thought I could win you back. I met Owen in one of his pubs and he was nice to me. I suppose we became friends. Then he told me that this young woman had arrived in Fairsands and he thought that you were keen on her. One of his mates saw you chatting in the shop and heard Phyllis invite you for supper. Owen encouraged me to follow you to Phyllis's. I wasn't going to do anything, but when you two were being so friendly and went off together I got angry and shoved the plant pot over before going on to the pub. Then another day when I turned up the door was open so I walked in and smashed the cake. I guessed you'd made it, Ellie, because of Phyllis's arm.

I admitted it. I wanted to get at you.'

'So the *he* you were talking about is Owen?' Ellie asked, wanting to be certain.

'Yes, he persuaded me to do things.'

'What do you know about the things that happened at the caravan site? You led us to believe you hadn't been there. Is that the truth, Amber?'

Amber looked down at her hands, then looked at Ellie. 'I messed up the caravan.'

Ellie glanced at Joe as he stood up and paced to the window.

Amber continued, speaking calmly and quietly. 'I've been very worried. At Phyllis's the door was open so it didn't seem like breaking and entering, but I broke into the caravan. I've been so scared of being found out and taken to court. All I wanted was to frighten you away, Ellie.'

'That was an awful thing to do.' Joe's voice was incredulous.

'I know, and I'm sorry. Truly sorry.' Amber wrung her hands.

'What do you know about the fire at the restaurant?' Joe asked.

'Nothing. I swear I had nothing to do with that.'

'What about the steps to the caravan?'

'That was nothing to do with me either. But . . . '

'You must tell us.'

'Owen told me he'd been at the site hoping to speak to Ellie when a noise startled him and as he tried to get away he tripped over the steps and dislodged them.'

'So what's all this for?' Joe indicated the belongings and empty suitcases.

'I'm going away. Well, *we're* going away. Owen has a business opportunity in Spain and he's asked me to go with him. It's all very sudden; he only heard from his friend yesterday. But it's a great chance for us — more than I ever dreamed of.'

Joe looked at Ellie and made a face. She knew they were both thinking the same thing: that it probably was too good to be true. But Owen and Amber would have to deal with that themselves.

Amber continued, 'So he's not interested in buying the caravan park or anything else in Fairsands. One of his mates is taking over the pubs and moving the administration of them to offices elsewhere. I'm sorry for Jane and the other staff losing their jobs, but I expect they'll be all right.' Amber's face lit up as she added, 'It seems incredible, but I've fallen in love again and Owen feels the same. I'm completely over you, Joe.'

Joe nodded.

'Will you tell the police about what I did?' Amber turned her attention to Ellie.

'I think we can overlook your act of revenge this time, Amber. You seem to have your future mapped out and I'm sure you won't repeat your unkindness on anyone else.'

'Oh, I won't, I promise. Thank you, Ellie, thank you.' Amber beamed with gratitude and gave Ellie a brief hug before picking up a pile of clothes and stuffing it in her case. 'But I thought Owen was coming round to see you. He said he wanted to tell you he was leaving and I thought he might explain that he was behind all the incidents, with me of course.'

'We saw him at the restaurant, but he must have chickened out. He made a quick getaway.'

'I don't suppose he's proud of himself. He's not all bad, whatever you two think. Anyway, I'd better finish packing. I don't want to miss our flight.'

'Good luck, Amber,' Ellie said as she made her way to the door.

'Don't think too badly of me, Joe.'

'I hope you'll be happy with Owen. Try and keep him on the straight and narrow.' Joe held the door open.

'I will. And thanks.'

As they walked down the path Joe took Ellie's hand. 'Phew, I think we need a breath of fresh air. Fancy a walk along the beach?'

Ellie didn't say a word as she squeezed his hand.

'I'm glad we know what's been going on,' Ellie said when they reached the beach. 'I hope it works out for them.'

'You have to be the nicest person ever. They've been really horrible to you and you want them to be happy!'

'No point wishing them ill, is there? I'm still wondering about the bike and the fire though.'

'I took a look at the bike with Mick and I'd say that was definitely wear and tear. It's pretty ancient and hasn't been looked after. I don't know about the fire, but I do believe that Amber and Owen weren't involved.' He reached down and selected a handful of flat stones. 'Skim some stones?' he asked, handing some to her.

They aimed flat, shiny pebbles towards the sea, counting the skims as the moon shone down on the two of them as they drew closer together.

14

'I hear Amber's gone off with that Owen. They deserve each other.' Phyllis passed a mug of tea to Ellie.

'It's awful for Jane who's been left in the lurch. She won't have a job.' Ellie bit her lip.

'Dear me, no. What will we do? Let's have a slice of cake and see what we can come up with. I made this myself with no help at all.'

Ellie smiled. 'Your arm looks much better.'

'It's almost normal and I think we can dispense with the rota. I hope people won't stop coming altogether, but I can manage most things now.'

'Hello, hello, hello,' boomed a loud voice at the back door.

'Come on in, Tommy. I knew you'd smell my ginger cake and be round.'

The policeman walked in and

settled himself on a chair. 'I've been looking for Joe. He wasn't in the restaurant or at the shop. Do either of you know where he is?'

Ellie didn't want to admit that she'd seen very little of him over the past week or so. 'I have an idea where he is, but if you leave your message with me I'll see he gets it.' Phyllis glanced at Ellie, but gave no explanation.

'I wanted to tell him about the fire. I caught some youngsters red-handed setting fire to the rubbish bins behind the school. After thorough questioning they admitted to a string of offences including setting fire to Joe's kitchen.'

'Well done, Officer,' Phyllis said as she raised her mug to him. 'Now pour yourself a cup of tea and have a slice or two of cake. You must be famished after all that hard work.'

* * *

'Nice humming,' Joe said as he came up behind Ellie and wrapped his arms round her.

'I'm happy in my work and I have a lovely boss.' She stacked the last of the tins and turned to face him. 'It would be nice if everyone had a lovely boss, don't you think?'

'You're after something, Ellie Montgomery.'

'It's just that Jane's lost her job.'

'I have been thinking about her.'

'Good.' Ellie gave him a peck on the cheek. 'You've got paint on your face. What have you been up to?'

'This and that. But about Jane . . . I think we can probably employ her almost full time. Not at Owen's great rates, but I'll do the best I can for her. I thought she could deal with the admin and accounts at the restaurant and the shop. That'll give Mum more free time when they come back. Vanessa said she needs someone to do the paperwork at the café too.'

'That's great. When will you tell her?

No one has seen her since Owen and Amber left and we think she's probably feeling upset.'

'I'll go and find her now if you'll promise to meet me at the restaurant as soon as Gwyneth comes in.'

'I promise.' Ellie started humming again as she tidied the packets of cornflakes.

★ ★ ★

Ellie jogged to the restaurant and found Joe taking a stock check of the bar.

'Ah, good. Now come with me.' He tucked her arm through his and led her once more to the door in the corner of the kitchen. The first thing that struck her was the front door, which was now painted in shiny blue gloss. Joe opened the door with a flourish.

'It's amazing. It's so light and cheerful now. Beautiful.'

'I thought if I painted the walls in light colours you could add your own colourful touches. I've bought basic furniture, but want you to put your own stamp on the flat. Hence the bare bulbs.' Joe gestured to the light.

Ellie wandered into the kitchen, which had been re-fitted. 'It's very nice, Joe.'

'Come and look at the bathroom too, and the bedroom.' He grabbed her hand and proudly showed her the two rooms. 'So what do you say? Will you take it?'

'I should think the rent has doubled with these improvements!'

'Please say you'll move in. I've been working really hard on it.'

'Of course I will. It's fantastic. And I'll be able to eat downstairs when I feel like it.'

★ ★ ★

'I'm disappointed,' said Phyllis.

Ellie was almost sure she saw Phyllis pout. 'Whatever do you mean? What have I done now?'

'You promised I could come to the

caravan for a meal with you and now you're moving out before I've visited. I've never been in a caravan before.'

Ellie dangled a bunch of keys in front of the older woman. 'It's still mine. I haven't moved all my stuff yet. I thought you wanted me to leave the caravan as soon as possible.'

'That's as maybe.' Phyllis sat on a chair in Ellie's flat, looking around. She sniffed. 'It's quite nice here, isn't it? You'll need lightshades. Those bare bulbs will hurt your eyes. And decent curtains, of course. I could come with you and choose some if you like.'

'Would you, Phyllis? Thank you.' Ellie smiled to herself, knowing Phyllis liked being brought to the flat and being the centre of attention. Ellie would arrange a picnic meal and they'd have a farewell to the caravan together.

'Where's Joe? No point me coming over to his place if he isn't here.'

'This is *my* place, Phyllis. Joe's place is downstairs.'

Phyllis put a hand on Ellie's arm.

'I'm only teasing you. It's lovely here and I'm pleased you decided to move in. Joe's made it look really cosy.'

'You knew he was decorating, didn't you, Phyllis? I thought he was avoiding me, but you knew what he was up to.' Ellie remembered the small niggle of uncertainty she'd experienced when Joe had been difficult to get hold of. She vowed never to doubt him again.

'Joe and I have known each other for a long while. I'm pleased he trusted me to keep his secret.' Phyllis stood up from the chair and wandered around the flat again. 'Now, have you got a tape measure?'

The meal in the caravan had gone splendidly. Phyllis and Ludo walked over and while the dog lolled outside in a shady spot, the two friends laughed their way through a delicious meal of pâté, bread, figs and tomatoes. Then Phyllis had brought out a bag and handed it over to Ellie.

'Phyllis, you shouldn't have. It's gorgeous.' Ellie carefully extracted a beautifully decorated cake. Iced, in lemon buttercream, across the top was, 'To Ellie'. It was such a sweet gesture, and the slightly off-centre wobbly writing made Ellie feel emotional. Blinking away a tear which threatened to spill, she bent and kissed Phyllis's cheek.

'I hope you've got a sharp knife. And we'll take a piece to Joe later, shall we? I think I'll have to let him know that I'm far too busy to consider working in the shop now. He did say to come back when my plaster was off.'

As they sat munching, Ellie said, 'I've been thinking about Joe.'

'I'm quite sure you have,' replied Phyllis, licking her lips and wiping her hands on the pretty serviettes Ellie had put on the table. 'About what in particular?'

'You prompted the idea, Phyllis, when you suggested coming here. I'd like to throw a party for Joe. He's worked jolly hard since I've known him, been generous with his time and energy, and has helped a lot of people.' Ellie's mind flew to Amber, Owen and Jane in particular, as well as to herself and Phyllis.

'When? What shall we cook? Who shall we invite?' Phyllis leaned forward, her eyes shining.

'I don't think we can do it on our own. We'll have to involve Joe, as it will be at his restaurant. With the best will in the world, there wouldn't be room here or at the flat.'

'His parents are coming home on Monday, which will be perfect, as that's the day the restaurant is closed. Shall we have it then?'

'Let's ask Joe.' Ellie didn't want to knock the enthusiasm out of Phyllis. It was good to see her fighting spirit, but if they were throwing a party, the restaurant was the best place for it and Joe would have to agree with the plan. Joe's parents? Ellie would have to meet them, of course, and she was sure they were delightful people. She just hoped she met with their approval.

'I'm so grateful to you and Joe for suggesting alternative employment for me. In a way I think it's worked out for the best. Once you got to know Owen, he wasn't too bad; quite kind really. But I only took the job with him for the money, if I'm honest. I loved working in the shop and now I'll be able to meet all my friends when I'm doing their books,' said Jane.

'I'm very pleased. By the way, Joe gave the go-ahead for a party at the restaurant as long as he isn't too heavily involved in the arranging of it. He's happy to do the cooking, but I don't see why he should do it all, do you? No good me offering as I'm a bit hit and miss. Phyllis has offered to make a couple of cakes and Vanessa will let us have some large cheesecakes and tarts. I could probably manage to toss a salad together if Joe did a couple of main courses. What do you think?'

'I think you're very well organised,

Ellie. I'll get some invitations printed. In fact I can probably get them done on the computer at home. Mick's quite clever at that sort of thing. And menus, I'll do them as well. Oh, this is so exciting. Let me make a list.'

★ ★ ★

The restaurant looked wonderful. Festive balloons and streamers festooned the interior, and there were flowers on the tables as well as rose petals scattered over the cloths. Ellie had planned the music. She hoped that Joe would sing during the evening, but hadn't asked him. She was sure he would need no encouragement in that direction.

Ellie looked up as she heard voices. A couple she didn't know had come into the restaurant and were staring at the decorations. 'Can I help you?' she asked. 'I'm afraid the owner isn't taking bookings for today. We're having a party.'

'It all looks wonderful,' said the

woman. Ellie liked her immediately. She was dressed casually and had a nice way about her. 'Are you Ellie? If so, I've heard an awful lot about you.'

'Yes, I am,' Ellie replied, extending a hand towards the couple. 'I'm afraid I don't know you. I'm a newcomer.'

'So are we. We've only been here for thirty years.' The woman laughed. 'We're Joe's parents. It's nice to meet you at last.'

'It's lovely to meet you. Joe's in the kitchen.'

But Joe was coming through the door with a big smile on his face. 'This is great. My favourite people together at last.' He enveloped his parents in a bear hug, which also managed to include Ellie.

'So what's been happening, Joe, apart from you meeting this pretty young lady?' asked Joe's dad.

'Not much, Dad, not much,' replied Joe, smiling at Ellie. 'Although you might be interested in some of the goings-on.'

Leaving Joe and his parents to catch up with each other, Ellie went back upstairs to change into her party clothes. She was pleased Jane had offered to go to the town with her and help her find something suitable for the evening ahead. She liked the reflection in the bedroom mirror and was glad she'd been persuaded to buy something in sea green. Twirling round, she hummed to herself; coming here and getting to know Joe and her other new friends had been the best thing she'd done. It would be nice to take a photo of everyone this evening and perhaps put it up on her wall.

Phyllis was one of the first people to arrive and she was soon followed by others. Ellie was introduced to people she didn't know and also got to know the names of several people she only recognised by sight from the shop. Many guests spoke to Mr and Mrs Baines.

Ellie gasped when Susan and her mum walked through the door.

'Surprise, surprise,' Susan said, as

she hugged Ellie.

'How wonderful to see you. I'm very pleased you're both here. How did you know about the party?'

'Phyllis, of course. She's obviously very much better and back to her usual ways, getting involved in everything.'

'She's very thoughtful. Come and sit next to me. I think it's time to eat. I want to hear all the gossip about people in the office.'

Susan smiled. 'I'm not surprised. Nothing ever happens down here, does it?'

Laughter filled the restaurant and the food was delicious. Joe had excelled himself once again by making a wonderfully rich and tasty beef stew as well as a lightly spiced chicken casserole. The potatoes dauphinoise were a meal in themselves and Ellie's salad added colour and freshness.

In order for the main course to go down and let people have ample room for the mouth-watering desserts on offer, someone put a CD on. No one seemed to have the inclination to dance, but then Joe's name was called out and guests took up the cry, 'Give us a song, Joe, give us a song.'

Joe sat on a high stool and began singing. His splendidly melodic voice entranced Ellie once again and she settled back to listen.

Feeling someone's eyes on her, she glanced round and saw Phyllis looking at her, a big grin on her face. Ellie smiled back. She couldn't believe how happy she felt. As the song ended everyone applauded loudly and there were shouts of 'more, more'. Joe shook his head, made his way over to Ellie, and took her hand. 'Ellie . . . '

'Time for the gifts now, Joe,' Phyllis interrupted. 'Let me have a seat and call the others over.'

Joe did as he was told and soon Ellie was surrounded by her friends with a pile of prettily wrapped gifts on the table in front of her.

'What are these for? It's not my birthday.'

'They're your flat-warming presents,'

Tommy boomed.

'How lovely.'

Gwyneth passed across a rectangular parcel. 'This is from Tommy and me.' Inside was a recipe book called *Foolproof Cakes*. 'Phyllis has taught you a lot about baking, we know, but we thought some recipes might be useful.'

Ellie flicked through the book looking at the colourful illustrations.

'Open ours now.' Vanessa passed over a much larger gift. 'Careful, it's breakable. I thought Chris was going to smash it on the way here.'

Ellie carefully peeled the paper away to reveal a beautiful three-tiered cake stand made from vintage plates. 'I can see that I'll have to invite you all to a tea party soon.'

Mick pushed across what was clearly a much heavier gift than all the others. Inside was a box containing a food mixer.

'I can't *not* make cakes now, can I? Thank you very much. It was too generous of you.' Ellie felt embarrassed that they'd spent so much money on her.

'It's not just a flat-warming gift, it's also a thank-you for helping me out with my employment problem,' Jane explained. 'We're going to be all right.' She squeezed Mick's hand.

'My turn now,' Phyllis said as she passed across her gift.

Ellie unwrapped a framed photo of Ludo looking lovingly at the camera. 'That's so sweet, thank you, Phyllis. Thank you everyone. This was supposed to be a party for Joe.'

'I'm glad you haven't forgotten me,' Joe said. Then he handed her the smallest gift so far.

It was a CD of Joe's music entitled 'A Feast of Songs for Ellie'. 'A mate helped me make it. He's in the music business.'

As the others chatted to each other, Joe took Ellie's hand for the second time that evening. 'Ellie . . . '

'Come and help yourselves to desserts,' Vanessa interrupted, and soon they were surrounded by people again.

After Ellie had enjoyed a large helping of banoffee pie and a chocolate fondant, which oozed a delicious runny middle, Joe took her hand. 'Ellie . . . '

'Now, Joe, I want to make an announcement. Quiet everyone.' Joe's dad banged on the table with a spoon. 'I'd like to propose a toast. To the success of Blue Horizon and to Ellie. We wish you every happiness in your new home.'

Glasses were raised and Blue Horizon and Ellie were toasted with enthusiasm.

Joe had a desperate look in his eyes when he grabbed Ellie's hand. 'Ellie . . . I want to tell you something, but each time I try something else happens. Will you dance with me, please?' he begged.

Ellie waited while Joe went off to put his CD in the player and when the music started they took to the floor. Joe put his arms firmly around Ellie and pulled her close to him.

'Listen to the words. This is what I've

wanted to say to you all evening,' Joe murmured in her ear.

Ellie glowed as she listened to Joe's voice. As the words of the romantic song flowed through Blue Horizon, Ellie heard Joe declaring his love for her and he did it perfectly. When the song ended, she kept her cheek touching his and relaxed against him. Then she remembered that they weren't alone and pulled away. The guests applauded loudly and Ellie was carried away on a sea of rapture as Joe planted a soft kiss on her lips.

THE END

We do hope that you have enjoyed reading this large print book.

Did you know that all of our titles are available for purchase?

We publish a wide range of high quality large print books including:
Romances, Mysteries, Classics
General Fiction
Non Fiction and Westerns

Special interest titles available in large print are:
The Little Oxford Dictionary
Music Book, Song Book
Hymn Book, Service Book

Also available from us courtesy of Oxford University Press:
Young Readers' Dictionary
(large print edition)
Young Readers' Thesaurus
(large print edition)

For further information or a free brochure, please contact us at:
Ulverscroft Large Print Books Ltd.,
The Green, Bradgate Road, Anstey,
Leicester, LE7 7FU, England.
Tel: (00 44) **0116 236 4325**
Fax: (00 44) **0116 234 0205**

ANNA'S RETURN

Sally Quilford

Anna Silverton and Janek Dabrowski escape war-torn Europe together, forging a friendship that carries them through difficult times. Even when they are apart, Anna dreams of Janek coming for her so they can be a family. Then, when she is accused of harming her half-brother, Teddy, she runs away, finding Janek again. Their childhood friendship soon turns to a tentative love, but the vicious lies told about Anna force them to part once again. Can the couple ever have a future together?